THE BALLAD OF JEW TOWN

Samyuktha Nair

olive turtle

NIYOGI BOOKS

Published by
NIYOGI BOOKS
Block D, Building No. 77,
Okhla Industrial Area, Phase-I,
New Delhi-110 020, INDIA
Tel: 011-26818960, +91 7428978881
Email: niyogibooks@gmail.com
Website: www.niyogibooksindia.com

Editor: Zinnia Sengupta
Design: Nadeem Ahmed
Cover design & illustration: Mohit Suneja

ISBN: 978-81-19626-96-0
Publication: 2024
Price: ₹350

This is a work of fiction. The names, characters and incidents portrayed in it are the work of the author's imagination. Any resemblance to actual persons, living or dead, events or localities, is entirely coincidental.

Printed at Niyogi Offset Pvt. Ltd., New Delhi, India

For my mother

Contents

Foreword

When Samyuktha first visited me at the synagogue I look after in Kerala, India—the Kadavumbhagam Synagogue of Ernakulam, the oldest active synagogue in the Commonwealth at 824 years old—the holy place was befitting of the nature of the meeting. She had approached me to learn more about the Cochini Jewish Community from me. I was instantly struck by the twinkle in her eyes, her brilliance and the impeccable interest she had in writing her fictional book in a way as real as possible. In fact, in the end, she has done it so well that this may even be considered a 'non-fiction novel', thanks to how real it is…

The Cochini Jewish Community consists of two distinct groups. The Malabari Jews, our older, earlier settlers who came from Iraq (Babylonia) and Yemen over 2000 years ago, and the newer Paradesi (white-skinned) Jews from Spain and Portugal, who came much more recently, after the Spanish Inquisition. Needless to say, the Malabari Jews have suffered great racism under the Paradesis, sometimes to unspeakable extents (more of which can be understood from the history book, *The Real History of the Cochin Jews Uncovered* by Thapan Dubayehudi).

Samyuktha's subtle and powerful story of a Malabari boy falling in love with a Paradesi girl and the rollercoaster of emotions and events that follows mirrors reality with a striking intensity. What follows is an unforgettable 'Abrahamic Adventure' spanning from Cochin to the moshavs and villages of Israel in its infancy in the 1950s.

This story will stay with you a long time. It not only opens your eyes to a new, unknown history in our corner of the world, but also leaves you satisfied by a beautiful tale, something rare nowadays. Enjoy.

Shalom.

Elias Josephai
Kadavumbhagam Synagogue
Ernakulam

Synagogue Lane

Cochin, 1950s

Yehuda stood at the head of Synagogue Lane, his eyes darting to the upper window of a large blue house. A thin lace curtain fluttered in the latticed window. He leaned against the wall, hands in his pockets, conscious of his appearance. His trousers were neatly pressed, his thin moustache freshly trimmed, and his curly hair tamed with a liberal amount of Brylcreem applied carefully before he left the house.

Most of the residents of Synagogue Lane were indoors, taking their afternoon siesta or listening to Malayalam songs on the radio. The few who had stepped out of their houses stared openly at the dark-skinned youngster. It was well known that Mattancherry's Jew Town was largely occupied by the fair-skinned Paradesi Jews, descendants of the Jews from Europe who had settled in Kerala in the 16th century. The older community of the Malabari Jews, who had long since integrated with the local population, lived across the backwaters in Ernakulam.

Their stares didn't bother Yehuda. His eyes fixed anxiously on the window; there was only one thing on his mind—Esther.

He checked his watch—it was half past four. She had been back from college for about an hour. He knew her routine by heart. Every afternoon, she and her girlfriends walked back from the nearby women's college, chattering, laughing, occasionally buying cotton candy from a roadside seller. They were a pretty sight in their cotton frocks and brightly coloured umbrellas, and Esther Zakiah was the prettiest of them all.

Esther lived with her parents and sisters, Hannah and Sarah, in their ancestral house on Synagogue Lane. She was the youngest of the three sisters, all of whom were guarded jealously by their stern businessman of a father and traditional Jewish mother.

Yehuda had first noticed Esther at a party thrown by one of the Malabari Jewish families in Ernakulam. Lounging against the wall with his friends, half his attention had been on the cricket scores emanating from the radio and the other half on the group of pretty girls dancing to the latest Elvis Presley record someone had procured from Bombay.

Her brown curls, her infectious smile, the slight gap between her front teeth, and her sparkling eyes held Yehuda spellbound. As she danced with the host (who was her classmate in college, he later learned), she was the very picture of innocence, completely unaware that Yehuda's heart had begun to dance with her, too.

Yehuda had approached her and they had struck up a conversation, exchanging the usual questions and answers—*What do you do? Where do you live?* And in her case, *who is your father?*

For it was essential that he knew just how deep in trouble he was. Losing his heart to a Paradesi Jew was dangerous enough, given the invisible lines of separation that stretched between the two communities, but the fact that her father was a rich businessman and one of the most influential elders of the community just drew the lines around beautiful young Esther Zakiah that much more firmly. She was off limits, destined to marry a rich Paradesi Jew like her father, and a dark-skinned chap from Ernakulam stood no chance of even going near her.

But he took the risk anyway.

***

The old Jewish wedding songs echoed down Synagogue Lane the night before Hannah Zakiah's wedding. Being the eldest, she was the first of the Zakiah sisters to get married. She was to wed the son of their neighbour, a wealthy businessman in his own right.

The match was perfect, as if sanctioned by Hashem Himself. Both the bride and groom were the eldest children of successful Paradesi merchants; both good-looking, with impeccable reputations. The women of Jew Town sang with gusto, the plaintive notes of their song extending to the open, light-filled windows of the neighbouring houses.

Yehuda parked his moped a few yards away from the edge of Synagogue Lane and switched off the headlight. Pocketing his keys, he smoothed down his dark hair and walked briskly towards the Zakiah residence. He took up his familiar post across the street, eyes fixed on Esther's window. The house was alive with music and it was clear that they had company. Esther's sister was probably being serenaded by her aunts and showered with bride gifts. During their brief meeting on the bridge earlier that day, Esther had told Yehuda that she'd be able to slip out for a few minutes when the others were distracted.

He checked his watch, and as if on cue, a lithe figure emerged from the back of the blue house, making its way silently to him.

Esther was dressed in typical Kerala Jewish attire—a sarong and a long-sleeved blouse, the latter richly embroidered. The powder-blue outfit complemented her pale skin, and her curls bounced prettily as she walked towards him. Yehuda's eyes softened as she approached, his thin face taking on a look of almost religious reverence.

She stopped a few paces away from him, a small smile playing about her lips.

'You look beautiful,' said Yehuda, feeling the warmth spread across his cheeks. Esther blushed.

'We are busy with the wedding preparations,' she replied, playing with the thin gold bangle at her wrist.

'Yes, I can hear the music,' replied Yehuda, feasting his eyes on her. He felt like he could look at her for years and still not get enough. It was so rare that he got a chance to stare unabashedly, to drink in her face. She was usually surrounded by her friends, and they could barely exchange a couple of words before she was whisked away.

'One day, the same songs will be sung for you,' said Yehuda, gesturing towards her house.

Esther raised her eyes to his. 'For Sarah first,' she said, referring to her other sister.

'Do they have someone in mind for her?' Yehuda asked.

Esther shook her head. 'Not yet. Father is usually the one who makes these decisions. He said he will start looking for a boy for her after Hannah's wedding.'

Her words filled him with an impossible sadness. After Sarah's wedding, Mr Zaklah would turn his attention to finding a groom for Esther, and Yehuda would definitely not be on the list.

Finally, he reached into his pocket. 'I have something for you,' he said, handing her a small packet, 'I hope you wear it at your sister's wedding.'

Filled with questions, her eyes met his, and she accepted the packet with both hands. Yehuda smiled.

'Read it when you're alone,' he said, 'I will wait for your reply.'

Esther looked intrigued, her gaze shifting from Yehuda to the package in her hands.

'See you tomorrow, Esther,' said Yehuda, taking one last, long look at her before disappearing into the darkness at the end of Synagogue Lane.

The Blue Rose

Esther wove her way through tables and chairs laden with drinks and sweetmeats, holding the packet firmly under her arm where it couldn't be easily spotted. The wavering voices lifted and dipped, weaving a centuries-old melody in her house, comparing the bridegroom to the legendary Joseph Rabban, the hero of the Cochini Jews, Paradesi and Malabari alike. It was all thanks to him that they had grown into a wealthy and respected community, and his name was carried down through the years, in song and story, as the ideal man.

Hannah was surrounded by their friends and relatives, a smile on her lips and a blush on her cheeks. A slightly older, plumper version of Esther, her hands were placed demurely on her lap, fingers adorned with gold rings that had been passed down through generations, from mother to daughter. Tomorrow, there would be one more ring—one that would be solely Hannah's—placed on her finger by her husband.

Esther gave Hannah a smile as she passed her and nearly bumped into her mother, who was carrying a tray of refreshments.

'Where are you going?' asked Mrs Zakiah, holding the tray high so that Esther couldn't knock anything off it, 'Come, sit with your sisters.'

'I just need to use the bathroom,' said Esther, dashing upstairs before her mother could tell her to use the downstairs one.

Once she was in her room, she shut the door and bolted it firmly before settling on her bed. The room, like the rest of the house, was done up in shades of white and blue—it had a large bed with pale blue sheets, a writing desk against the window, where a pair of lacy white curtains fluttered slightly in the breeze, and a massive old armoire where Esther stored her clothes and other little treasures.

Unwrapping the packet with quick, slender fingers, the first thing that slid into Esther's palm was a dainty, sparkling brooch. It was in the shape of a rose, dotted with tiny, glittering blue stones. She turned it over, noting the delicate, elegantly crafted pin at the back. The brooch had clearly been purchased from one of the many shops lining the seaside at Fort Cochin. While it was obviously not expensive, it was exactly the kind of thing she liked, and she was surprised that Yehuda had selected her gift with such accuracy.

Setting the brooch carefully on her pillow, she pulled a folded sheet of paper out of the packet. Holding it to her nose, she took a deep breath. It had the faint fragrance of

Yehuda—of the salty sea spray and the cool, moist air that caressed his face as he rode his light-green moped to Synagogue Lane to meet her.

Smiling, she opened it, thrilled at the sight of his neat, mature hand.

My dear Esther,

What I am about to say is probably not a surprise to you. I have been seeking you out for more than two months now, and we have been exchanging smiles and speaking to each other whenever we get a moment alone.

Nevertheless, I would like to make my feelings clear: Esther Zakiah, I have fallen in love with you. I cannot go a single day without seeing your sparkling eyes and beautiful smile—they warm my heart like nothing else, and stay in my memory long after you have departed.

When I was in Fort Cochin with my friends, this brooch caught my eye. It was placed in the window of a jewellery shop, as if waiting for me to find it. It immediately reminded me of you, and I decided it had to be yours.

Esther, if you reciprocate my feelings, please pin this brooch onto your dress when you go for your sister's wedding tomorrow. I will be nearby, waiting to catch a glimpse of you.

With love,
Yehuda Avraham

A small smile on her lips, Esther held the letter to her heart as she picked the brooch off her pillow, turning it so the blue stones caught the light and winked up at her.

***

The next morning, Yehuda and his friends reached Synagogue Lane bright and early. They weren't the only ones. The entrance to the street was crowded with onlookers—dark-skinned children with skull caps and big, kohl-lined eyes, fishermen in checked lungis, and youngsters like him—all eager to catch a glimpse of the wedding festivities of renowned businessman Benjamin Zakiah's eldest daughter.

A troupe of drummers had been hired for the event, and they stood at the head of Synagogue Lane, dressed in their pristine white mundus, drums resting against their legs, secured by a thick strap that went around their necks. The rhythmic beats of the *chenda* filled the air, resonating in Yehuda's chest as he peered restlessly through the throng, sometimes standing on tiptoe, trying to catch a glimpse of Esther.

As if on cue, the wedding party emerged from the big blue house. First came Benjamin Zakiah and his wife. Zakiah was dressed in his best suit, his embroidered kippah poised carefully on his balding head. His spectacles shone and his chest was puffed up with pride. He smiled at the gathering like a king greeting his subjects, his queen beaming on his arm. Plump little Mrs Zakiah was in a heavily embroidered blouse and sarong, a small handbag swinging from her arm as she walked beside her husband, her gold jewellery glittering under the sun.

Next came the bride, dressed in pristine white and shimmering gold, her translucent veil giving the audience a glimpse of her perfectly coiffed curls. Her fitted blouse was embroidered with a profusion of tiny golden beads, with her skirt grazing the toes of her narrow shoes. She was flanked by her sisters, both in identical cream dresses.

Yehuda only had eyes for Esther. Her head bowed slightly, she smiled at Hannah, a hand on her elbow as she led her out of the house with Sarah. Her curls were adorned with cream roses, and the skirt of her dress flared out at the hips, stopping below the knee, giving him a glimpse of her smooth, slender legs.

On the creamy fabric covering her breast glittered a tiny, rose-shaped brooch.

Cigarettes by the Sea

After the wedding procession entered the Synagogue, Yehuda and his friends peeled out of the crowd, riding their mopeds to the Fort Cochin beach to enjoy a lazy Sunday morning. It made no sense to wait outside the Synagogue till the ceremony was complete; they might as well enjoy themselves. Despite the relentless work of Abraham Barak Salem—the freedom fighter who had spent his life fighting for equal rights for the Malabari Jews, and his son's marriage to a Paradesi Jew—it was difficult to change the mindset of an entire community. Malabaris entering the Paradesi Synagogue was something that was still frowned upon by the community's older, more conservative members.

Yehuda worked at his father's electronics shop in Ernakulam. While they weren't *wealthy* like many of the Paradesi Jews, the shop made enough to support the family of four—Mr Avraham, his wife, Yehuda, and Reena, Yehuda's younger sister.

Yehuda took a deep drag from a cigarette before passing it on to his friend. The group was settled on the sand, thin trousers rolled up, the water licking their bare toes. The beach was calm, undisturbed by the few tourists who were dipping their toes tentatively in the water and the balloon seller who was stalking them.

Yehuda observed the tourists. They were clearly a married couple from up north—the salwar kameez-clad woman was wearing the red wedding bangles that were characteristic of a Punjabi bride, and the man had a long beard and wore a turban, the usual markings of a Sikh. The woman shrieked as a wave splashed the bottom of her salwar, then broke out laughing, clinging tightly to her smiling husband's arm. Yehuda's mind wandered back to Synagogue Lane, to the wedding that was taking place there at that very moment.

As if reading his mind, his friend Jacob said, 'I heard Benjamin Zakiah is throwing a big party for his daughter and her husband after the wedding,' and blew a plume of smoke towards the water.

'He certainly has the money for it,' chuckled Aaron, 'Did you see the gold on his wife?'

'I suppose it's only a matter of time before the second one gets married, and then they'll start looking for a groom for Yehuda's girl,' said Sam slyly, giving Yehuda a sideways glance as he accepted the cigarette.

Yehuda kept his face smooth, waiting for Sam to take his drag and pass the cigarette to him.

'I'm not so sure about that,' he said coolly, leaning forward to accept the slowly diminishing cigarette.

'Why, are the Zakiahs going to let their daughters marry us, now? I thought they considered us a different species,' said Sam, his face hardening.

Yehuda took his time to reply, blowing a stream of smoke in his friend's direction. Extinguishing the butt in the sand, he pulled a cigarette packet out of his pocket and told his friends about the letter, brooch, and Esther's acceptance as he lit another one. Aaron accepted the newly lit cigarette, but continued to stare at Yehuda, his eyes wide.

'That girl has more guts than I thought!' he said, 'So does this mean you're going to ask for her hand in marriage?'

Yehuda leaned back on his palms, feeling the warmth of the sand between his fingers.

'I need to discuss it with her first, but yes, eventually, I plan to,' he said.

***

Yehuda returned to Synagogue Lane that night, parking his moped a safe distance away before proceeding to the blue house he had grown to be so familiar with. Its windows were bathed in golden light and music poured out of them, along with the aroma of traditional Cochini Jewish food. The party was clearly in full swing.

Yehuda leaned against the wall of a neighbouring house, heart racing, waiting for Esther to slink out and meet him, as had been their nightly routine for the past two weeks.

Punctual as always, she soon slipped out of the back door and made her way towards him. Yehuda straightened up, flattening his hair with his palms.

Dressed in a light pink sari and sleeveless blouse, Esther was wearing light makeup that accentuated her delicate features. She smiled as she approached him, and his heart leapt when he saw that his brooch was pinned to her chest.

There was a moment of silence as he basked in her gaze, the golden glow in his heart expanding to fill his entire body.

'You look so beautiful,' he said in a low voice. Esther dipped her head, offering him another one of her heartbreakingly endearing smiles.

'I wore the brooch all day,' she said softly, her eyelashes grazing her cheeks.

His heart hammering, Yehuda decided to be bold.

'Does that mean you love me, too?' he asked huskily, stretching out his hand. When Esther slipped her slim one into his, he felt like he was soaring.

Looking up at him with innocent, trusting eyes, she simply said, 'Yes.'

Confession

Yehuda was twenty-four years old, a good four years older than Esther. He had become a man the moment he had started working at his father's shop, and was proud of the honest labour he put in to earn his modest income. Yehuda indulged in the occasional drink and cigarette but was neither a drunkard nor an addict. He prided himself on the quiet control with which he held his baser desires.

He stood in front of the mirror, carefully parting his clean, oiled hair. Combing his thin moustache with the small plastic comb he carried around in his back pocket, he exhaled deeply, giving himself a once-over.

The lines of his sleeveless vest were visible beneath the pale cotton of his shirt, and his trousers were neatly pressed and creased. Despite the powder he had dabbed under his armpits, he felt himself begin to sweat when he thought of the task ahead of him.

Not task. *Tasks.*

Stepping out of his small bedroom, he walked over to the drawing room, his breath catching in his throat as he took in the sight of his parents and sister.

His parents were sitting on the threadbare sofa, his mother in her nightdress. She was peeling vegetables quietly, her knife making quick, dexterous movements. As a child, Yehuda had always thought that women like his mother would make excellent warriors—they knew their blade like the back of their hand. However, they chose to turn their weapons to vegetables and meat instead, cooking up a storm for their families.

His father—thin, with a receding hairline and a skinny moustache identical to his son's—sat beside her, legs stretched out before him and wire-rimmed spectacles perched low on his long, bony nose as he frowned at the Malayalam newspaper. Yehuda had often been told that he was the spitting image of his father, minus the deep lines that bit into the older man's high forehead, forming soft grooves on his skin.

His sister, on the other hand, strongly resembled their mother. With her round face, full lips, and long, oiled braids, she looked exactly like the Hindu girls she went to school with. Her Jewishness showed through only when she spoke, revealing an extensive Hebrew vocabulary mingled with her daily Malayalam. Reena was sitting on the floor, bent over her textbook, no doubt studying hard.

Yehuda stepped closer to his family, clearing his throat slightly. His father looked up from his newspaper, the lines on his forehead staying in place as he looked his son up and down.

'Going out?' he asked, taking in Yehuda's more formal clothes.

Before Yehuda could respond, his mother said, 'If you are, I have a list of things I need you to pick up for me.'

Yehuda shook his head. 'No, Umma, Bava—I'm not going out. I just wanted to talk to you.'

His father raised his eyebrows, exchanging a glance with his wife.

'About what?' he asked, folding his newspaper in half and leaning forward with the air of someone preparing to hear a great secret. And in a way, he was. 'I can't remember the last evening you spent with us. Usually, you go off somewhere on that moped of yours the minute you get free from work. I hope you're not doing anything…unnecessary.'

'No, Bava,' said Yehuda, moving to stand in front of his parents, 'I'm not. It's…'

His gaze shifted to his mother, who nodded, her eyes wide with curiosity.

'I like a girl,' he blurted out, immediately cursing himself for how clumsy, how childish it sounded.

He should have chosen his words better, sounded more mature and dignified. Instead, he had confessed his love like an awkward schoolboy. Yehuda felt a hot flush spreading over his cheeks.

His father's brow contracted.

'Which girl?' he asked, sitting straighter on the old sofa.

This was the hard part.

Yehuda took in a silent breath, his eyes locked on his father's as he said, 'Esther Zakiah.'

***

The next night, as Yehuda got off his moped and turned into Synagogue Lane, his eyes automatically sliding to the first floor of the blue house, he saw that Esther was already leaning out of her window, waiting for him. The moment she saw him, she disappeared from view, and a minute later, slipped out of the back door and made her way to him.

'So, what did they say?' she asked breathlessly. Yehuda studied her face—nervousness was written all over her big eyes, slightly furrowed brows, and the straight line of her mouth.

'It was as we expected,' he confessed, taking her hand in his, 'They were…horrified. Not so much because of you, but because of your…father.'

Esther nodded, dropping her gaze to his collar. Benjamin Zakiah was widely known for being one of the more conservative members of Jew Town, to put it mildly. He believed that the white Jews were the true Jews, the ones with Solomon's blood running through their veins, the true inheritors of Joseph Rabban's legacy. He saw the Malabaris as nothing less than converts; simple, native Keralites, with no legacy to claim. Yehuda's father was one of the many Malabari Jews who scorned the beliefs of Zakiah and others like him. They firmly believed that it was them, the Malabaris, who had come to this land in the times of Solomon, carrying the legacy of Joseph Rabban in their veins, their dark skin ultimate proof of the fact that they far outdated the Paradesi Jews in Kerala.

'But,' continued Yehuda softly, 'I know they will support us, when it comes to that. My father believes the Malabaris and the Paradesis should be treated the same—and that extends to marriage. As long as I find a good, Jewish girl—which I have—I know he will support us.'

A small smile touched Esther's lips, but the worry didn't leave her eyes.

'Now, *I* need to speak to *my* father,' she said with a small sigh, turning to look at the blue house over her shoulder.

***

Esther had spent days planning how she would speak to her family about Yehuda, and decided to tell them on the

Shabbat, after the morning visit to the synagogue. Since a visit to the holy place usually left her father mellow and benign, she felt that it was a good time to strike.

As Esther readied herself for the synagogue on Saturday morning, she realised that it would be the first time in her life that she would be walking down the narrow road to the tall, ancient Paradesi Synagogue without Hannah. Ever since she was born, it had been a family ritual to walk together to the synagogue—starting off with baby Esther balanced on her mother's hip, and Hannah and Sarah holding their father's hands. Now that Hannah was married, she would be going to the synagogue with her husband's family, sitting with them, and would probably be able to interact with her parents and sisters only after the service was over.

Esther smoothed down her pistachio-green dress and peered into the mirror, running a comb through her curls. As if on cue, there was a soft knock at the door.

Sarah peeped in through the crack, dressed in a blue frock, Siddur and purse in her hand. Like Hannah and Esther, she, too, had the trademark brown curls, slight figure, and bright brown eyes they had inherited from their mother.

'Ready?' she asked.

***

During the Shabbat service, Esther tried to lose herself in prayer and ignore the bubbling pot that seemed to have inhabited her belly, threatening to spill over. Her sisters sat on either side of her—calm, and blissfully oblivious to her nervousness. Hannah's husband's family had decided to sit with the Zakiahs, and Esther was glad to be seated between her sisters, just like old times. As the families made small talk in the sun-dappled street outside the synagogue, Esther twisted her handkerchief nervously, bouncing on the balls of her feet.

'What happened to you?' asked Hannah shrewdly, observing her sister from beneath her wide umbrella, 'You seem jittery today.'

'I'm not, I just need to use the bathroom,' lied Esther, glancing at the clock tower beside the synagogue. Hannah gave her a sympathetic smile. 'It's good that the house is so close by,' she said, 'You'll be able to go soon.'

Marriage suited Hannah. She had seamlessly transitioned from the virginal, obedient Jewish girl to the happy housewife, a look of proprietary contentment in her soft brown eyes as her hand rested in the crook of her handsome husband Ezra's arm, her wedding ring glinting in the sunlight. She wore just a hint of lipstick, and a thin, gold chain glittered around her neck. She looked like a younger version of their mother, embarking on the first steps of married life.

Esther smiled. 'I hope you're happy?' she asked quietly, glancing at her sister's in-laws, who were chatting with her parents.

'I am,' said Hannah, exchanging a loving smile with her husband that said it all. Her journey through life had been smooth—she had married the man of her parents' choice, and was now a young wife, blessed with the approval of her in-laws, and the good wishes of the entire community. Esther knew that things would be very different for her and Yehuda.

***

Once they got home, Esther went into the downstairs bathroom and closed the door, letting out a deep breath as she listened to the familiar sounds of her mother bustling around, her father settling into his favourite armchair to peruse the newspaper, and Sarah cooing at the birds in the verandah, whom she fed on a daily basis.

Esther turned on the tap, splashed her face with the sun-warmed water, and took a few deep breaths as she wiped her face with a soft towel, her heart fluttering like a bird. Picturing Yehuda's smiling face, she opened the bathroom door, deciding not to prolong the wait.

Damp palms flat against her skirt, Esther called out to her mother and sister in a slightly quavering voice, asking them to come to the drawing room. Her father looked up from his newspaper, his brow furrowed.

'What is it, Esther?' he asked, his voice slightly stern. Benjamin Zakiah liked his household to run like clockwork, and anything out of schedule—even on the day of rest—irritated him.

Esther gave her father a nervous smile, watching her sister peep in from the verandah. Her mother emerged from her bedroom, divested of her handbag and in the process of removing her pearl earrings.

'Please sit down,' said Esther, her voice cracking slightly. She cleared her throat, dabbing her white handkerchief against her forehead.

Her mother and sister exchanged glances as they settled side by side on the sofa, facing her. Benjamin Zakiah put away his newspaper and removed his glasses, giving his youngest daughter a piercing look.

'Go on,' he said, immediately making her feel like she was the one summoned before him, ready for a cross-examining.

Esther licked her lips. She had gone over various ways to begin the conversation, each opener sounding weaker than the next. Finally, she had decided to be direct, but polite—to make her point without sounding like an impatient child who just wanted to get her way.

'Mama, Papa,' she began, trying her best to keep her voice level, 'I want to marry Yehuda Avraham, from Ernakulam.'

The Light at the End

Yehuda waited impatiently at the entrance to Synagogue Lane. He glanced at his watch—ten minutes had passed. Esther had never been late before. He wished he could just walk up to her house and knock on the door—it ached to be so close, yet so far.

His eyes kept darting to the first-floor window, whose curtains were pulled firmly shut, blocking any light from spilling out onto the street. He kept hoping Esther would come to the window, or give him some indication as to what was keeping her.

Sighing, he leaned against the brick wall of the house behind him. It belonged to the Israels, who, given the darkness that shrouded the building, were already fast asleep. They were an elderly couple whose children had been part of the first wave of the migration of Indian Jews to Israel. While their children had packed up and left to pursue the Zionist dream a few years prior, the old couple couldn't bring themselves to say a permanent goodbye to their leafy, rainy motherland—Kerala.

Opportunities for Indian Jews were plentiful in Israel. It was a country that was starting over and calling upon Jews of all nationalities to join hands and reclaim their 'fatherland'. Initially, there had been some concern doubt about taking in Cochini Jews, since there was a fear of them carrying over filariasis from their wet, mosquito-ridden homeland. This fear had since abated, but once they got to Israel, the Cochini Jews were settled in the dry, arid Negev—the desert—just in case.

On the day of Hannah's wedding, when Yehuda and his friends had lounged about on the beach at Fort Cochin, Aaron had expressed a desire to make *aaliyah* to Israel.

'I want to be a part of it all,' he had said, gazing into the distance as he held the half-smoked cigarette between his fingers, 'I want to work, to serve in the military, to be one of the people who builds the new Israel.'

'It won't be so easy, brother,' Sam had said, 'After living in Kerala, with a regular monsoon, enough food to eat, and a comfortable, predictable life, how are you going to carry a gun and walk for miles in the desert?'

'With faith,' Aaron had responded simply.

Yehuda was jerked out of his thoughts by a sudden movement in the blue house. The curtains of Esther's window had been jerked open, and golden light poured out of it onto the street below. Yehuda hurried to the front of the house, looking up at the window, his heart racing. He knew Esther wouldn't leave him hanging. But why hadn't she come downstairs?

A pale face appeared at the window. Esther looked down at Yehuda with an unreadable expression that immediately created a knot in the pit of his stomach. She didn't even smile.

Glancing over her shoulder, she dropped a small package into the street, and quickly drew her curtains again. Yehuda stared up at the window where she had stood, his brows knitted in confusion. Taking a few steps forward, his hand closed around the small package. When he turned it over, he saw that it was an envelope tied to a stone.

Yehuda wasted no time in ripping it open.

Dear Yehuda,

I am sorry that I am unable to meet you today. I told my parents about us, and they didn't take it well at all.

My father threw a fit and gave me a lecture that lasted over an hour. He believes that I am going to spoil his name in the community, and make our respectable family a laughing stock—these were his words, not mine. When I told him that according to Jewish law, all Jews are to be considered equal, irrespective of the colour of their skin, he slapped me for talking back to him.

I've been locked in my bedroom, and have no permission to leave the house except to go to college—and Sarah is to escort me to and from there so that I don't make any 'detours' on the way.

My family is not speaking to me, but don't worry—I will be fine. They haven't told Hannah about my wanting to marry you, because they don't want her in-laws to get a 'bad impression.'

Yehuda, I promise you that I have not given up. We knew we had a fight ahead of us—this is just the beginning. Come to Synagogue Lane every night as usual—I will throw a letter out of my window every day, so that you are aware of everything that happens.

I love you.

Your Esther

Yehuda looked up at Esther's blank window, his face burning with anger. His fingers gripped the delicate paper of the letter tightly, crumpling it. How dare they cage his beautiful, sweet Esther? How dare they slap her, simply for telling the truth?

His fingers trembled as he folded the letter and placed it carefully in his breast pocket, close to his heart. As he walked back to his moped, shaking with rage, he promised himself that he would free Esther from her cage.

***

'They locked her up?' asked Jacob incredulously.

'Yes,' replied Yehuda gruffly, refusing the cigarette that was passed to him. He was in no mood to smoke—to distract himself in any way—till he had got Esther out of that godforsaken house.

Aaron reached for the cigarette, his brow furrowed.

'I had heard Zakiah was strict with his daughters, but I didn't know it was this bad,' he mused, blowing out a stream of smoke over the still waters.

The friends were sitting at the edge of the pier at Fort Cochin, gathered under the star-studded sky, the upturned, tarpaulin-covered fishing boats keeping them company.

'What did you expect?' asked Sam sardonically, taking a deep puff from the dying cigarette, 'After his eldest was married off with pomp and splendour to a rich white fellow, is he going to allow his youngest to run away with one of us?'

'No one said anything about running away,' snapped Yehuda, 'We have not committed any crime. We want to get married properly, in a synagogue, with our families present.'

'It won't be in the Paradesi Synagogue, that's for sure,' said Sam, passing the cigarette to Jacob.

***

On Sunday afternoon, Esther was lying on her bed, curled up on her side. The rose brooch glinted on her open palm, catching the harsh, white glare of the electric light above and turning it into a pleasant twinkle. There was a soft knock on the door and Esther sat up, pinning the brooch to her chest as she did.

Sarah peered around the edge of the door. 'May I come in?' she asked.

Esther shrugged, feigning indifference as she picked up a discarded textbook and leaned against her fluffy pillows. Her final exams were coming—she was nearing the end of her degree—and she tried her best to study in those few hours when she could calm herself enough to focus on things other than her father's rage and the seeming hopelessness of her situation.

'I'm not your enemy, Esther,' said Sarah gently, entering the room. Sitting on the bed, she faced her younger sister, who was still studiously ignoring her.

'I brought this for you,' she said in an attempt to break the stony silence. Esther looked up from her textbook to see her sister slide a chocolate towards her, a hopeful look in her eyes. Esther didn't accept it, but she put down her book with a sigh. Sarah's eyes went to the brooch glinting on her chest.

'Did he give you that?' she asked, nodding at the piece of jewellery, 'I noticed you wearing it at the wedding.'

Esther stuck out her chin in defiance. 'Yes, he did,' she said tightly.

Sarah looked at her, the expression in her eyes halfway between sadness and compassion.

'Don't be so short with me, Essie,' she said softly, using Esther's childhood pet name, 'I, too, wish that Papa wasn't so angry. But that's the way he is—he still has that old mindset that Paradesi Jews are, well…'

'Are above the Malabaris,' completed Esther in a hard voice, 'which is complete nonsense! On the one hand, Papa talks about how his ancestors came over from Spain about five hundred years ago, and on the other hand, he says we are ancient Jews, settled in Kerala since the time of King Solomon! How does that make any sense?'

Sarah sighed. 'Yes, it makes no sense,' she agreed, 'But to argue with Papa on these matters will only make things worse. Right now, you need to focus on studying for your exams. Don't they start on Monday?'

'How can I study when I'm locked up like this?' asked Esther bitterly, slamming her palm down on the bed, 'I'm being treated like a prisoner!'

Sarah bit her lip. 'I know, and it's not right,' she said in a low voice, 'I don't think you've done anything wrong.'

Esther stared at her sister. 'You don't?' she asked.

Sarah shook her head. 'I don't believe in all this Paradesi-Malabari nonsense. We are all Jews—that should be enough.'

Before Esther could speak, Sarah continued, 'However, there is no point arguing with Papa. He is very orthodox.'

Esther's shoulders slumped, and she began worrying her thumbnail with her teeth. Sarah gently eased her hand away from her mouth.

'So what should I do?' asked Esther, her forehead creased in worry.

Sarah leaned forward, and said in a conspiratorial whisper, 'I have an idea.'

***

That night, when Yehuda reached Synagogue Lane, he was surprised to find Esther's window open and waiting. His heart lifting ever so slightly, he hurried towards it, face upturned, silvery raindrops landing on his dusky skin. Esther was waiting for him, her elbows resting on the white window sill, a smile on her face.

Yehuda exhaled, gazing up at her. He had no idea what was going on, or how they would work their way out of the mess they were in, but he knew he could spend a lifetime worshipping at her altar, doing whatever he could to ensure that smile remained on her face. She was his hope, his salvation—she made him want to be a better man, just so he could be worthy of her.

Esther disappeared from the window, and reappeared with a small package in her hand. Yehuda knew immediately that it was an envelope tied to a rock. She aimed carefully, and when she threw, he caught it nimbly, all those years of playing cricket with the boys of Ernakulam paying off. Flashing her a smile, he quickly undid the package and opened her letter.

My dearest Yehuda,

My sister, Sarah, supports us. However, I request you to keep this fact private, in case our father finds out.

She will be escorting me to and from my exams, starting tomorrow. Please meet us at the Fort Cochin pier at 3 pm—my exam will be over by then. Sarah has thought of a plan which we would like to share with you.

All my love,
Esther

Yehuda kissed the letter, and smiled up at Esther broadly, not caring that the rain was pelting down on him ferociously, soaking through his thin yellow shirt and plastering his hair to his head. His heart sang, and his eyes filled with tears of happiness. He was grateful for the rain—he didn't want Esther to see him crying. From the window, she blew him a kiss.

The Plan

'I'm going out, I'll be back soon,' Yehuda told his father the next afternoon.

The pair was at work, Avraham bent over the accounts book while Yehuda attended to customers.

Their relationship had been somewhat strained since Yehuda had announced his plans to marry the daughter of a man who was well-known for considering the Paradesi Jews to be superior to the Malabaris, and who frowned upon Malabari Jews setting foot in the Paradesi Synagogue.

Nevertheless, Yehuda continued to remain steadfast, riding over the pang he felt when his father pursed his lips, or gave him a disapproving glance. *I am marrying Esther, not her father*, he said numerous times, to no avail. As far as Avraham was concerned, the Zakiah family was to be kept at arm's length.

Yehuda grabbed the keys of his moped, trying to ignore his father's pointed stare as he strolled out of the shop, hands in his pockets. He whistled, trying his best to appear nonchalant. Once he was out of his father's line of sight, he hopped onto his moped, and sped off towards the Fort Cochin pier.

***

Esther stood at the pier with her sister, the wind whipping their hair and dresses about them. She clutched her books to her chest, occasionally glancing at her watch through narrowed eyes, trying to keep out the sand that stung her face. Her knees wobbled slightly, but she forced herself to remain standing, to show Sarah just how utterly confident she was about Yehuda.

A familiar light-green moped swung into view, and Esther let out a deep breath as she watched Yehuda park it, pocket the keys, and jog towards the pier.

'They're not very well-off, are they?' asked Sarah under her breath, taking in the dilapidated moped.

Esther shot her a look, and Sarah retreated.

Yehuda bounded up to them, taking a moment to catch his breath. His eyes roved over Esther, softening at her earnest gaze, but became guarded when he took in her sister. He inclined his head at Sarah politely, clearly not sure what to say.

'We don't have too much time, as our parents mustn't suspect that we stopped somewhere on the way home from college,' began Sarah, getting straight to business, 'As Esther has told you in her letter, I support the two of you. I think this division between the Paradesi and Malabari Jews is ridiculous.'

Yehuda gave Esther a small, surprised smile, and she reached for his hand, giving it an encouraging squeeze. However, aware of her sister's gaze, she retracted it quickly.

Sarah took a deep breath, steeling herself for what she was about to say. She knew that once she had conveyed her plan to Yehuda, there would be no going back. And she had to make sure her parents never found out that it was her idea.

Holding Yehuda's gaze steadily, she said, 'I know of a way the two of you can get married.'

***

A week passed by quietly in the Zakiah household, with Benjamin managing his flourishing business, his wife, Miriam, looking after the home, and Sarah escorting Esther to and from her exams. Benjamin still wasn't talking to Esther, and while she was no longer confined to her room, she wasn't allowed to step out of the house alone, lest she go to meet 'that boy from Ernakulam'.

'They're not even well off!' snorted Benjamin one evening, easing his leather shoes off his feet after a long day of work, 'I've seen him going around on that ancient moped—they don't even have a car! How are they going to look after Esther? She's used to a certain lifestyle.'

Esther, who was studying at the dining table, gritted her teeth. She knew she was meant to hear this little speech directed at her mother, and her knuckles whitened around her pen. Meanwhile, Miriam tried to ease the tension. 'I got some fresh fruits today, why don't you try them?' she asked, bustling out of the kitchen with a tray. This was how Miriam Zakiah always dealt with difficult situations—while she rarely knew what to say to the aggressors, she knew that the sight of fresh food could stall even the worst of tempers.

As she passed the dining table, she rested her hand briefly on Esther's shoulder—a silent gesture of comfort. Esther closed her eyes, on the verge of tears. How she wished she could just sink into her mother's familiar, perfumed embrace and be a child once more. This conflict had drawn fault lines across her family, and Esther felt like she could no longer talk to her mother. Kind as Miriam was, Esther feared the possibility of her relaying the news to her husband in her undying domestic obedience. She stared at the page of her textbook, eyes blurring with tears. What she and Yehuda were planning would only serve to further widen the gap between her and her parents, but her father's attitude left her no choice.

***

On Friday, Esther set her pen down as the bell rang shrilly through the classroom. Several girls let out sighs of relief, flashing each other triumphant smiles. They were finally done with their undergraduate exams, and those who passed would be conferred their bachelor's degrees. Esther knew she would pass. English Literature had been her favourite subject since school, and it came naturally to her. Her father's exacting need for perfection had made all three of his daughters diligent students—another feather in the family cap to be enthusiastically discussed at community parties with the other Paradesi Jews.

Esther watched the invigilator move efficiently between the aisles, collecting the answer sheets. Her knees trembled beneath her desk. Now that her BA exams were over, it was time to execute Sarah's plan.

***

'Since Esther's exams are over, maybe we should have something special for dinner today,' said a smiling Miriam Zakiah that afternoon, 'Sarah, ask her to come to the kitchen, will you? Let her decide tonight's menu.'

Sarah, who was sitting at the dining table with a book, bit her lip. It was time to play her part. Setting down her Malayalam novel neatly on the table, she smoothed down her dress, going up the stairs obediently. However, at the landing, she turned towards her room, not Esther's.

Opening her capacious wooden cupboard, Sarah inhaled the familiar scent of freshly laundered clothes scented with rose petals as she reached far in, stretching her arm all the way to the back. Her nails scraped against the wood at the back of the cupboard and made contact with a thick envelope.

Taking it out, she waited for a moment, taking a deep, grounding breath before heading back downstairs.

'Mama, Esther is not in her room,' she said, arranging her features into a mask of worry, 'I found this letter on her pillow.'

White Roses and Worry

Esther glanced at the entrance of the Malabari Synagogue near Yehuda's house, wondering if her family would attend. In her letter, she had stated that she did not wish to elope and get married in secret, and had cordially invited her family to attend her wedding, giving them the exact time and place. As Sarah took the letter, she had said that while she would love to attend, it depended on Mama and Papa—if they chose not to and she defied them, it would raise suspicions that she had been part of the plan.

Esther smoothed down the puffy skirt of her simple white dress, feeling her palms turn slick with sweat under the satin gloves. Her heart hammered wildly in her chest; on the one hand, she was so close to finally marrying Yehuda—the man she loved with all her heart—and on the other, she was praying her father wouldn't storm in and snatch her away, or do anything else to disrupt the wedding.

Yehuda's family, surprised and rather disconcerted by the impromptu wedding, had turned up nevertheless. It was his sister who had helped Esther get ready, and his mother who had handed her a simple bouquet of white roses sourced from a nearby florist. The two women looked at Esther curiously, a hundred questions in their eyes.

'Are you sure, *mole*?' Mrs Avraham asked as she adjusted Esther's skirt, 'You and Yehuda are adults, and we cannot stop you from following your heart. But we don't want any problems from your family.'

Esther reassured her with a smile that didn't quite mask her own worry. 'Like you said, Aunty, we are adults. My family won't cause any problems. Don't worry.'

She checked her watch. It was time to head to the Kadavumbhagam Synagogue.

Flanked by Yehuda's family, she made the short walk from his house to the entrance of the synagogue, trying her best to ignore the stares of the neighbours gaping at the white Jewess getting married in their place of worship. She felt their gaze boring holes into the white wedding dress she and Sarah had hurriedly procured. There had been no time to get a traditional Cochini skirt, blouse, and veil made the embroidery would take time, which was something they didn't have.

The only people invited, apart from their respective families, were Yehuda's friends—Jacob, Aaron, and Sam. Esther had decided against inviting any of her college friends—dear as they were, they often came over to her house, and there had been the risk of them informing her parents about her plan.

The ceremony was simple and quiet. Esther found herself unable to look away from Yehuda's warm smile, love and pride burning in his eyes when he saw her in her wedding dress. When he slipped the simple gold wedding band that had once belonged to his grandmother onto her finger, Esther felt an overwhelming sense of peace that washed away the anxiety that had made its home in the pit of her stomach ever since she'd handed the letter to Sarah.

However, when she turned to face the small gathering of guests, a smile on her face and her hand in her husband's, her eyes couldn't help but linger on the empty seats which were meant for her family.

***

After spending a blissful night at a modest hotel in Ernakulam, Esther and Yehuda headed to Synagogue Lane on Saturday morning. Esther sat sideways behind Yehuda on his trusty moped, her wedding ring catching the sunlight from where her hand was resting on his shoulder. She had chosen to dress simply in one of the few dresses she had brought from home. Before leaving her house, she had packed a small collection of her most practical dresses, footwear, and a few saris into a single suitcase, which Sarah had smuggled to Yehuda as he waited in his usual spot outside the house on the night before the wedding. She hadn't been able to move all her belongings out of her room, lest her parents suspected something.

As the scooter sputtered to a stop outside her house, Esther glanced at the windows of the neighbouring houses nervously, wondering if any nosy neighbours were lurking, waiting to get their claws into the family drama brewing under the roof of the very respectable Mr Benjamin Zakiah. So far, they remained curtained with lengths of delicate white lace, typical of Jew Town houses.

The curtain of her own living room shifted, and Esther saw Sarah peer through. A moment later, her sister hurried through the door.

'Everyone is here, even Hannah,' she said urgently, 'They're very upset. There's not much time for a conversation before we go to the Synagogue.'

Esther glanced at Yehuda, who squeezed her hand.

'Was Papa very angry?' she asked in a low voice. Sarah's eyes darted between the newly-wed couple, and then to the ring shining on Esther's finger.

'Yes,' she said softly, 'I'm sorry, Essie. I really wanted to attend your wedding.'

'But it would have looked suspicious if you had disobeyed Papa to go,' completed Esther, 'I understand.'

There was a moment of silence before Yehuda took a deep breath and said, 'So shall we go in?'

The Walkout

As Sarah announced their arrival in a tentative tone, Yehuda and Esther slipped off their shoes, leaving them at the entrance of the house. They walked into the living room, where they were met with stony stares and a silence so thick it could be cut with a knife.

Esther gave the room a quick once-over. Sarah stood against the bookcase, nervously chewing at her thumbnail. Anxiety radiated off her in waves, her brow knitted as she waited for someone to speak. Hannah was seated on the sofa beside her husband, her eyes wide as she took in Esther and Yehuda. Her husband's handsome, usually open face was unreadable.

Hannah's in-laws were sitting on the two armchairs, their expressions grave. Her plump mother-in-law, with her exquisite clothes and glittering diamonds, was openly giving Yehuda a disapproving stare. He responded by squaring his shoulders and standing even taller.

Esther's eyes finally focussed on her parents. Her mother was clutching the back of a chair, knuckles white, her eyes full of tears. Her father, already dressed for synagogue, was looking at her, his face hard, eyes like chips of stone.

Esther cleared her throat.

'Hello, Mama, Papa. This is my husband, Yehuda Avraham.'

***

An hour later, Esther's ears were still ringing. She clutched Yehuda's hand tightly for support as they walked the short distance from her house to the Paradesi Synagogue, well aware of the disapproving glares of the elders boring into their backs. Yehuda's face was pale, his lips pressed together, and in that moment, despite the turmoil raging in her heart, Esther had never felt more at one with him.

Hannah's mother-in-law had been the first to explode.

'What has your daughter done, Miriam?' she shrieked at Esther's mother, 'She has spoilt her life! Ruined the name of your family!'

Esther felt blood rush to her face, and she longed to cross the room and slap the older woman.

Yehuda, seeming to sense this, squeezed her hand—a silent signal urging her to stay calm. So Esther settled for throwing her sister's mother-in-law the most scathing look she could muster. But now, the woman's scandalised gaze was on Esther's and Yehuda's joint hands.

'Why did you do this, Esther?' asked her mother tearfully, 'How can we go to the Synagogue now?'

Esther's temper flared again.

'With your head held high,' she said in a clear voice, doing her best to keep it steady, 'According to Jewish law, all Jews are equal in the eyes of God. Yehuda's family have been Jewish for hundreds of years. I don't see what the problem is.'

'Don't be so idealistic, child—' began Hannah's father-in-law, in a gentler tone than his wife, but Esther's father cut him off.

'You have damaged more than just your reputation,' he said coldly to Esther, not even bothering to glance in Yehuda's direction, 'You have ruined the family name, our standing in society, Sarah's chances of finding a good husband… Your childish adamance will have you excommunicated by our entire community. How will you survive? Stupid, stupid girl.'

Esther could feel Yehuda's body go taut, every muscle trembling with tension. She wished she could apologise to him on behalf of her family, to ask his forgiveness for the way they were treating him, as if his Malabari heritage made him someone not worth knowing, not worth interacting with. As if he was someone beneath the fair-skinned, light-eyed Paradesis.

'I have married an honest, kind man who loves me,' said Esther, her voice trembling, 'Survive? I will *thrive*.'

The elders in the room exchanged glances, clearly thinking Esther naïve and foolish. However, Yehuda gave her a small smile, his eyes full of love. He faced her family, and cleared his throat.

'I know our communities have their...differences,' he said carefully, trying his best to rein in the part of him that wanted to point out just how wrong they were to the privileged, white-skinned men and women who were doing their best to avoid his gaze. But he had to be polite, for Esther's sake. 'But I request you to give me a chance. I love Esther very much, and intend to keep her happy for the rest of her life.'

Esther's mother gave him a quick, anguished look before turning to her youngest daughter.

'The two of you are speaking like naïve children,' she said, 'Once you start facing problems, your idealism will fade.'

Esther gritted her teeth. Her parents simply could not look beyond money.

With the tension growing thicker than ever, Hannah's father-in-law cleared his throat delicately and peered at his watch, hinting that they set out for the Synagogue. Since Esther and Yehuda were still standing near the door, they were the first to leave.

When they reached the Synagogue, Esther found several members of the community giving her and her husband pointed looks. Their eyes seemed drawn to the back of Yehuda's thin shirt, the dark skin of his neck visible above his pale collar, his black hair curling against it. As they had decided, Yehuda and Esther ignored the stares, and proceeded to remove their footwear before stepping onto the cool, tiled floor of the Paradesi Synagogue.

As Esther proceeded from the small anteroom to the inner chamber, followed closely by Yehuda, she was stopped. One of her neighbours, a wealthy, middle-aged businessman much like her own father, stepped in front of her. His eyes were fixed on Yehuda.

'You can't come beyond this point,' he said, 'If you would like to pray, sit at the back.'

'The back?' asked Esther indignantly, 'Why? I always sit with my family.'

'Things have…changed now,' he replied, crossing his pale, hairy arms across his well-fed belly and giving Yehuda a pointed look. Esther's back straightened.

'I don't see how,' she said coolly, sidestepping him to take her usual seat at the front. After a beat, Yehuda followed her, taking a seat, for the very first time, in the Paradesi Synagogue.

There was a shocked silence in the hall. Esther looked straight ahead, but Yehuda raised his eyes to the gallery, and was met with pursed lips and wide eyes.

One by one, the white Jews got up from their seats, shuffled out of their rows, and left the Paradesi Synagogue, till only Esther and Yehuda were left in the old, sunlit room.

Aaliyah

In the month that followed, Esther settled in with Yehuda and his family in their modest home in Ernakulam. She helped his mother with the household chores and ran errands by day, and slept curled up beside her husband on the ancient double bed in his childhood bedroom by night, the moonlight filtering in through the small windows with their horizontal metal bars, typical of the houses of the area.

While they had all the basic amenities in place, Esther found her life vastly different from what it was on Synagogue Lane. She was no longer the coddled youngest daughter of a wealthy household, spending her carefree days with her friends and attending parties by night, dressed in pretty frocks.

She was a woman who contributed to the household, who cooked, cleaned, and sometimes went to her husband's shop to help him. Fortunately, her mother had ensured that Esther and her sisters had learnt all the traditional Cochini Jewish recipes to prepare them for married life.

If she was being honest, she would have admitted to herself that while her new life wasn't difficult, it wasn't easy, either. She was used to having all her free time to herself, to read a novel, meet her friends, or spend time with her sisters. To be so busy that the only time she had to herself was the few minutes before she fell asleep every night was a strange feeling.

Her respect for her in-laws rose as she saw how hard they worked to run a household without the multitude of servants she was used to. They weren't poor, of course, but they had to work hard for a living. There were wealthy families among the Malabari Jews, too—running restaurants and hotels and other big businesses. It just so happened that Yehuda's family was not one of them.

As they lay in bed that night, cuddled under the cotton sheets, Yehuda gave Esther a gentle smile, his eyes full of love.

'You have no idea how much I admire you,' he said softly, tucking a lock of curly hair behind her ear.

Esther wrinkled her brow, settling herself more comfortably against the pillow.

'Admire me for what?' she asked, trailing a finger across Yehuda's thin cheek, feeling the sharp spikes of the stubble that appeared every evening against the soft pad of her finger.

He sighed. 'Living here can't be easy for you, can it?' he asked bluntly.

'What do you mean?' asked Esther, not quite meeting his eye. Yehuda slid a finger under her chin, and gently raised her gaze to his.

'You are used to luxury,' he said simply.

Esther stared at him defiantly. 'I love you,' she said firmly.

Yehuda rested his hand on her cheek, the calluses warm against the soft coolness of her skin. His eyes were tinged with something unreadable…not quite sadness…was it regret?

'I know, Esther,' he said gently, 'I love you, too. And I will make a better life for you. For us. I promise.'

***

Every day, Esther crossed a date off the Malayalam calendar that hung on the wall of the small room she shared with Yehuda. Every day, she put away a few rupees in a small, flat box she kept in the old cupboard that was home to all their clothes.

She was saving up, just like he was. Ever since they'd decided to get married, they had known that life wouldn't be the same for them—especially not for Esther. They would become an oddity, to be stared and pointed at, to be discussed in hushed tones at parties by smug elders holding their glasses of liquor, shaking their heads in disapproval at the rash behaviour of the young. They knew that to expect the Paradesi Jews—especially the more traditional ones—to drop their prejudices against the Malabaris overnight was asking too much. Esther would forever be considered the woman who married beneath her, and Yehuda would always be regarded with suspicion.

It was for this reason that they had decided to emigrate, to start afresh, to go to a land where they would be equal, and where the colour of their skin and their ancestry wouldn't be brought up as a dinner table debate every single evening. They had decided to emigrate to Israel.

***

Two months into their marriage, Esther was standing at the small sink in the kitchen, scrubbing the steel vessels the family had just had their lunch in, when she heard the familiar *put-put-put* sound of Yehuda's moped spluttering to a halt at the front gate.

Peering out through the kitchen window, she saw him hurrying excitedly to the front door, a thick envelope in his hands.

Curious, Esther turned off the tap, and pressed her hands against the soft, worn cotton of her checked apron as she headed to the living room to greet him. Her father-in-law was still at the shop, and her mother-in-law was taking her afternoon nap. Reena, of course, was at school. So Esther was the only one to greet Yehuda when he suddenly decided to return early from work—something completely out of character for him.

As soon as she opened the door, Yehuda beamed down at her, before picking her up and kissing her full on the lips.

'Yehuda!' she exclaimed, her cheeks red, looking over his shoulder at the houses across the street to see if the neighbours were watching. However, her husband was beyond caring.

'Pack your bags, my love,' he said gleefully, waving the envelope in her face, 'It's time to make *aaliyah*! I've bought our flight tickets to Israel!'

Israel

'To make aaliyah' is a Jewish term which means 'to return to the fatherland', Israel.

After World War II, thousands of Jews from around the world packed their bags and travelled to Mandatory Palestine, where, under the British mandate, the land had been recently bifurcated into Palestine and Israel. They were hoping for a fresh start, a better life, in the land of their spiritual forefathers. After years of persecution at the hands of the Nazi Party, it was something of a relief to have the chance to establish a country they could call their own, where they were in the majority, where they were safe.

India was one of those rare countries where Jews had no history of persecution. They had flourished there for centuries, as a small but wealthy and respected community—running businesses, hospitals, schools, getting educated, and holding posts in the public sector and government. Tourists, especially from the West, were always amazed to find little Jewish clusters tucked away in various parts of India, thriving quietly and peacefully, and never failed to document them.

This was how Jew Town had become famous—drawing in photographers, writers, professors, and historians to marvel at its rich and rare culture, and to spread the word about this quaint, beautiful little township nestled in the heart of Kerala, amidst swaying coconut trees and the Arabian Sea.

Esther peered out of the window as the plane got closer and closer to land. As the clouds thinned, she could see a vast expanse of desert getting closer, dotted with sparse vegetation and a few scattered buildings. Her first impression was of a land under construction, and she couldn't help but make a mental comparison to Kerala—lush, blooming, and absolutely nothing like this sun-beaten desert.

Yehuda, who was seated beside her, was also looking out of her window, his expression unreadable as he took in the new, unfamiliar landscape. Esther studied his face. There were dark circles under his eyes—no surprise there, he had barely slept on the entire journey. It was his very first time on a plane, and he had displayed a quiet, bright interest in the airport, in the interiors of the plane, in the existence of the meticulously groomed air hostesses (though he tried his best to hide it).

Yehuda's eyes had stayed wide open through it all, taking in everything with a childlike innocence that Esther found incredibly endearing.

As she watched the thinning clouds reflected in her husband's eyes, his gaze shifted to hers, his wide eyes softening.

'What are you thinking?' she whispered, careful to keep her voice low in the quiet interiors of the aircraft. Yehuda smiled.

'I am thinking…that this is incredible. Amazing. It's… exhilarating to travel, and to fly.'

Esther smiled at his rare display of emotion, squeezing his hand on the arm rest between them.

'You made this possible,' she reminded him gently, 'This new life, for both of us.'

Yehuda squeezed her hand back, his eyes ardent. 'I pray our life here will be good,' he said.

***

Like many Cochini Jews who had migrated to Israel, Esther and Yehuda were settled into a transit camp. A barren field filled with tents, it offered the most basic of amenities, and served as a shelter for new immigrants who hadn't been allotted housing yet. There were Jews of all nationalities living in the tents, making use of the communal bathroom and kitchen, where volunteers cooked food for them thrice a day. There was also a small medical tent, equipped to provide basic care.

They were told that housing would be allotted on a first come-first serve basis, but Yehuda noticed that white-skinned Jews were given preference. The authorities stared him down when he questioned them indignantly, and Esther pulled him away by the hand, not wanting to make trouble.

The tent was cold at night, and very, very far removed from the comforts of Cochin. Esther found herself dreaming of the old bed in Yehuda's room, with its proper mattress and blankets. She developed rashes on her legs from the sand that somehow managed to creep into their bedclothes and irritate their skin, and got herself a tube of ointment from the medical tent.

The communal bathroom was dirty, and smelt terrible. The tent-dwellers were repeatedly asked by the authorities to clean up after themselves, but not everyone did. Yellow stains were everywhere, and it wasn't rare to see fat black flies buzzing around the toilet. Esther absolutely hated using it, and prayed they would be allotted a house soon.

Finally, she and Yehuda were relocated to a small, square, whitewashed house in a moshav in the Negev. A moshav was an agricultural settlement, where several Zionist settlers who believed fervently in working together to build up the promised land, to use their own hands to restore it to its lost glory, lived and worked together.

For the first few months, Yehuda worked on the land with several others. Some farmed, some reared animals—he was a goatherd, spending long hours out in the sun, watching his charges graze on the wilted grass. For the first time in her life, Esther was running her own household, and it took a little while for her to come to terms with the amount of housework she had to do. At her parents' house, she had lived a pampered existence with servants to take care of all the cooking, cleaning, and gardening. At her in-laws', she always had the help of Yehuda's mother and sister. If she had thought she was tired at the end of the day back then, it was nothing compared to how she felt at the end of the day in her new life in Israel. However, she thought, glancing at her husband as he slept deeply, snoring beside her, Yehuda definitely had it worse.

Yehuda's already slim frame was now even slighter, the hollows of his cheeks visible under his sharp cheekbones. His dark skin was tanned, resembling burnt sienna under the unforgiving sun, courtesy of the long hours he spent grazing goats during the day. Esther had initially thought she would be lonely during her long hours alone—this wasn't like Ernakulam, where the shop was close to their house, and he could come home for lunch on slow days.

However, she needn't have worried. Several young wives like her—many of them Cochini migrants themselves, from both Synagogue Lane and Ernakulam—helped her settle into her new life, set up her small house, and even earn a wage by herself while her husband was at work.

Together, a group of Cochini women set up a small food business—too tiny to be called a restaurant, it was more of a catering service to help foster a sense of community among the Cochini families, to make them feel at home. Esther began to enjoy her days in the company of the friendly, chatty women—some of whom she had known in her childhood before they emigrated—and took pride in the smiles on the faces of the Cochini families when they savoured the delicacies she had made with her own hands for their modest weddings and birthdays in the barren Negev.

Months passed, and like several young, able-bodied men, Yehuda was enrolled in the Israeli military. The first time Esther saw him in uniform, she felt a lump in her throat. It hung slightly on his thin body, but she could not deny the pride that shone in his eyes as he saluted her. He, along with several young men, was assigned to border patrol.

While Esther was home alone for weeks, re-reading his letters before she slept at night, tears sparkling in her eyes as her hand rested on her ever-growing belly, Yehuda spent night after night trudging through unfamiliar terrain, ever-conscious of the loaded gun he carried.

As he stared at the midnight sky that seemed to stretch endlessly over the horizon, something in him tugged at his heart—some long-buried, unheeded part of him that whispered, *Cochin was not like this.*

Miriam

Years later, Esther would remember her first pregnancy as the loneliest period of her life. Yes, she had the ladies from work keeping her company during the day—buzzing around chattering, fussing over her as her belly grew. Esther insisted on working till the very day she went into labour—sitting alone in the empty house with only her thoughts for company was utterly depressing. She preferred to work—time seemed to pass by more quickly when she was busy.

Ever since her last disastrous visit to Synagogue Lane, she had fallen out of touch with her family. They had not reached out to her, and her pride didn't allow her to contact them either. What would she say? *I'm lonely? I wish you were with me?* Any sign of weakness would be taken as their triumph, and she would not, under any circumstances, let them think she was anything less than happy.

She was happy—more or less. Happy to be Yehuda's wife, happy to be expecting her first baby, happy to be working and doing something productive with her time…yet, a deep loneliness gnawed at her, making her heart feel like a stone in her chest when she slept alone at night, looking at Yehuda's empty, unwrinkled pillow bathed in moonlight.

She wrote to her in-laws often, and they wrote back regularly. Through them, she was sure that news must have spread to Synagogue Lane that she and Yehuda had emigrated to Israel and were expecting their first child. Yehuda's friends wrote often, too, and Esther enjoyed laughing at their light-hearted tales. Sam was planning to migrate to Israel, too—he thought that job opportunities would be better there, and he might even find a nice Cochini girl to marry. He hadn't set a date yet, but Esther found herself looking forward to his arrival—it would be like the old days again, at least to a certain extent.

More than anything else, she ached for her sisters and parents. She found that her anger at her father had dimmed over the months. Yes, she still firmly believed that he was wrong in his prejudices against the Malabaris, but he was also her father, and two decades of memories weren't easy to wipe out.

She also missed her gentle mother, whose plump, fair fingers would pull her youngest daughter's cheeks as she laid a steaming dish before her, and whose hearty, infectious laugh would set everyone off around her at their lamp-lit evening parties.

She dearly wished she could talk to her sisters again, to have Hannah and Sarah support her through her pregnancy, make her laugh and smile with their absurd gossip and girlish jokes, and just hold her hand when she felt lonely and unbalanced by all the hormones. Her mother-in-law had given her the news of Hannah having delivered a baby boy a couple of months earlier—a fair-haired, chubby child named Benjamin—Ben for short, after their father.

That night, Esther had cried her heart out into her pillow, wishing with all her heart that she could speak to her sister, and at least see her new nephew in a photograph.

Of course, she never told Yehuda of her crushing loneliness. She ensured that her letters to him were nothing but sunny and cheerful, filled with amusing anecdotes from life in the moshav, and assuring him that she was doing just fine. She had absolutely no desire to cause him any guilt—with relations tense between Israel and Palestine, she could only imagine the pressure he was under, and had no intention of distracting him with further worry.

One winter day at work, she was sitting placidly at the small table the ladies had set up, her swollen feet resting on a stool as she prepared dough for the spiral Malabar parottas that were in great demand among those homesick for Kerala, when she felt a sudden wetness on her seat.

Looking down, she saw the wetness spread through the skirt of her dress and realised, with a distant, almost disconnected jolt, that she was going into labour.

Mere hours later, she was lying in a hospital bed, holding a small bundle in her cannula-fed arms. The Cochini women had stepped up, taking her to the hospital, speaking to the doctors, assuring Esther that giving birth was nothing to be afraid of, and that it would be over before she knew it. Esther appreciated the company, but she wasn't afraid. She felt a curious detachment from the entire thing, as if she were watching herself being wheeled into the operation theatre on a TV screen.

By virtue of her youth and good health, the delivery was quick, and Esther could barely recall it as the days went by. It all seemed like a blur—the blue hospital walls, the doctor's masked face, the nurses asking her questions and noting down her mechanical answers, and the motherly Cochini women, bringing her food and smiles and clean clothes from home, cooing over her new baby and marvelling at her big eyes and soft curls.

The child was an unusual combination of Esther and Yehuda—she was fairer than her father, but darker than her mother. She had jet-black curls and light eyes that looked exotic in her small, brown face. Her coral lips were full, her lashes long, and her forehead high.

'Look at her! She was born for the desert,' joked a plump Cochini matron who had come to visit.

Esther smiled faintly, looking down at her bright, inquisitive daughter. The girl was already showing signs of curiosity and intelligence—traits no doubt inherited from her hard-working father. Esther closed her eyes for a moment, willing herself not to cry in front of her visitor as her heart ached for Yehuda.

'What are you going to name her?' asked the kindly woman, leaning over to tickle the baby's chin.

'Miriam,' said Esther immediately. During her pregnancy, she had been consumed with thoughts of her family—especially her mother. Over the months, the choice of name had become blatantly obvious.

'After her grandmother,' explained Esther, summoning all her self-control to prevent her voice from cracking.

Surviving

Esther sat in her easy chair at home, a small smile playing on her lips as she read Yehuda's letter. She had sent him pictures of Miriam; he wrote that he kept them safe in his wallet, just like he did with Esther's pictures.

Esther wiped away a tear that had made its way down her cheek, the words on the paper blurring over. Yehuda's letter was filled with so much love that it made her heart ache.

She glanced at Miriam, sleeping peacefully on the bed. Her plump lips were wrapped loosely around her tiny thumb, and Esther had to resist the temptation to smother her with kisses lest she disturb her sleep. Once Miriam woke, it was notoriously difficult to get her to go back to sleep.

The emptiness of the house weighed heavily on Esther and she made a decision on an impulse.

Reaching over to her nightstand to grab her pen and letter pad, she opened a fresh page and did something she hadn't done in months.

Uncapping the pen, she wrote: *Dear Mama, Papa, and Sarah…*

***

Weeks had passed since Esther had posted her letter, but there had been no response. She had written the letter with butterflies in her stomach, and had been on tenterhooks ever since she had posted it. She didn't know what she was waiting for. Was she hoping for a long, tearful letter from her family, welcoming her back into the fold, their hearts thawed by the enclosed photograph of Miriam? And if they did, was she ready to forgive their prejudices towards Yehuda? How would Yehuda feel about it? Would he see it as a betrayal? Of course, he was too nice to stop her from reconnecting with her family, but deep down, would he feel a twinge?

Esther was distracted, confused—all she wanted was some comfort. It had been several months since Yehuda had been able to come home on leave and no matter how hard she tried, she couldn't find happiness and fulfilment in looking after Miriam all by herself.

She had the help of the other Cochini ladies, of course, many of whose husbands were in the armed forces themselves. They were kind, but she could never bring herself to talk to them about the loneliness that gnawed at her. She was afraid it would make her look strange, or cold—how could a mother not find complete fulfilment in her child? Was there something wrong with her?

Esther buried her head in her hands, bitter tears falling from her eyes, staining the soft, pale blanket covering her baby.

***

In a couple of months, Esther resumed her duties at the Cochini food joint. She took Miriam to work with her, and the little girl was getting spoilt silly by all the indulgent, motherly women and sweet Cochini girls who delighted in carrying her, pointing out things to her, and generally making much of her. They were a close-knit community, and Esther had no worries regarding Miriam's safety—several pairs of kindly eyes watched her like a hawk, and some of the other ladies started bringing their children to work, too, so the little ones always had each other for company.

The Jewish community in the Negev grew larger as more and more families emigrated to Israel. There were African Jews, Asian Jews, American Jews, and hundreds of Holocaust survivors from Europe. Old habits were hard to let go of, and it took a little time for the more conservative Cochini Jews to mingle with those from other countries. However, the youngsters mingled with more ease, and Esther found herself in awe and admiration of the brave men, women, and children who had survived the Holocaust. They were regaining their health and rebuilding their lives, but the shadow of those terrible years of persecution had not quite left their haunted eyes. Nevertheless, they worked hard and displayed extraordinary resilience, utterly grateful for their lives and their homeland—Israel.

Esther often found herself reflecting on how lucky she was to have grown up Jewish in India. India was one of the few countries in the world which had never persecuted Jews—rather, it had treated them with respect and acceptance. Esther had known comfort, safety, and privilege all her life, and had never considered herself or her loved ones at risk for being Jewish. Kerala was a place where Hindus, Muslims, Christians, and Jews had lived in harmony for centuries—they worked together, played together, and studied together. It had always struck Esther as strange that the only divisions and prejudices were the centuries-old faultlines between the Paradesi and Malabari Jews.

In Israel, it did not matter. They were a diverse nation, with Jews of every nationality, race, and socio-economic background. In this new setting, with this infant society working hard to build itself, the old prejudices of Synagogue Lane seemed even more absurd to Esther—they seemed like words written in a long-forgotten diary, fading to the back of her mind as she got to know her neighbours better, and grew used to the fact that her past privilege based on claimed ancestry and skin colour did not make her special here.

Letters from Home

Yehuda had come home on leave, and Esther was thrilled. His presence lit up the little house, and Esther found her old energy coming back as she bustled around to cook his favourite dishes and clucked over how skinny he had become.

It made her heart overflow to see Yehuda with Miriam. He held her carefully, like she was made of glass, and spent hours watching her with a look of adoration and reverence in his eyes. He crawled with her on the floor, let her take naps snuggled against his chest, and even got up to pacify her when she woke up cranky in the middle of the night.

Miriam somehow seemed to know that Yehuda was her father. The first time he held her, she didn't fuss or cry or reach out to Esther as she normally did while meeting new people. Instead, she simply stared at him with her big, bright eyes, sucking her thumb placidly.

Eventually, she began to laugh in his company, his antics and funny faces bringing out a little gurgle of laughter that delighted both her parents. Countless pictures were clicked, dozens of family walks and picnics planned, and Esther found herself going to bed with a smile each night. Now that her Yehuda was home—even though it was for a short while — her lonely, aching heart was at peace.

***

The week before Yehuda returned to duty, Esther received a letter with an Indian stamp, bearing her name and address in very familiar handwriting.

Her heart hammering, she ripped it open, wondering if her wishes had really come true.

My dear Esther,

I am sorry I couldn't write earlier. Mama and Papa were being extremely difficult, one of them accompanying me wherever I went, making it very hard for me to go to the post office alone to send you this letter! I suppose they were afraid that I had some secret lover tucked away in Ernakulam, and would run away when their backs were turned.

However, I can finally move around in peace now, because I'm engaged. Yes—you read that right—despite all their silly fears of not being able to find a good match for me, my engagement actually worked out fine.

The boy is Adam Eliyahu, the eldest son of Mr Eliyahu—owner of the Fort Bay Hotel. Do you remember him? He used to attend synagogue with us before he went abroad. He's just come back from England, where he read law. He's got a job there, and his parents wanted to find him a nice Cochini girl while he was on holiday in India. And guess who they chose?!

Our engagement was a week ago—I'm enclosing a picture for you to see. We've been spending time together since, dining at restaurants, and taking long walks along the Fort Cochin beach. Since Mama and Papa are no longer afraid of me running away, I can go out on my own now, and was finally able to send you a letter! I'm really sorry for the long gap, Essie—I hope you forgive me. Now that I'm freer, I will be writing to you much, much more often!

My dear, I just want to hug and congratulate you and Yehuda from the bottom of my heart on Miriam's birth! I cried when I read the letter—I wanted to drop everything and catch a flight to Israel to be with you and my new niece! She looks so round and lovely—a perfect combination of you and Yehuda! I keep her photograph under my pillow with little Ben's (Hannah's son, born not too long before Miriam), so that I can look at both my niece and nephew before I sleep at night.

Mama cried when she heard you've named the baby after her, and wanted to write to you, but Papa stopped her. Papa and

I had a row about it, but he didn't budge. Sometimes I wonder if he has a lump of coal for a heart.

However, I showed your letter to Hannah, and she and her husband want to resume contact with you. I gave them your address—I expect you'll be getting a letter from her soon. I'm glad our generation doesn't seem to share the same stupid prejudices as our parents!

Give the baby the biggest hug and kiss in the world from me. I wish I could do so in person! Convey my love to my brother-in-law. I can't wait for your reply!

All my love,
Sarah

Wiping her tears, Esther examined the photograph that had been carefully folded into the letter. Sarah was dressed in a new sari, the light chiffon and sleeveless blouse perfectly setting off her slim figure. At her side was a young man dressed in a light suit, his hair neatly combed off his forehead. He had a strong nose, and while he was not handsome in the traditional sense, there was something warm about his smile that Esther immediately liked.

Kissing her sister's picture, she took the letter inside to show Yehuda.

***

A few days later, Esther received a letter from Hannah. Her eldest sister was deeply apologetic for hesitating to support her, and admitted it was because she was afraid of jeopardising her relationship with her new in-laws. Her mother-in-law was a rigid woman who laid extreme importance on 'maintaining their image' in society, and Hannah found herself at a crossroads—falling in line with her mother-in-law and turning her back on Esther, or supporting Esther and risking her marriage.

Though she had initially chosen the first option, she wrote that she was eaten up with guilt—it just didn't feel right to shun her own sister for marrying out of the community. A Jew was a Jew—why did it matter if he was Malabari or Paradesi? The more she thought about it, the less sense the narrow-minded beliefs she had grown up with made to her. The final piece fell into place when she decided to discuss the matter with her husband.

Since they had had something of an arranged marriage, it had taken a while for the formality to completely wear off between Hannah and Ezra, and for them to completely bare their hearts to each other. However, her pregnancy had brought them much closer, and had broken away the last of the careful propriety in their relationship.

Ezra had admitted that he, too, felt that his mother was being unnecessarily narrow-minded in her approach to

Esther's marriage, and that he was coming to believe that the divisions between the Paradesi and Malabari Jews—divisions he hadn't even thought about while growing up, were actually more likely to harm the collective Jewish community in Kerala than do any good.

'With so many Jews migrating to Israel,' he had told Hannah, 'There might come a time when the Cochini community is so small that only marriages between the Malabaris and Paradesis will keep us alive. These divisions will just push us to our end.'

I am ashamed that it took a conversation with my husband for me to fully understand that you had done nothing wrong, Essie, Hannah wrote, *I understand if it takes you time to forgive me. But I promise you, sister, I will never turn my back on you again.*

Cochin Calling

Over the months, letters flew back and forth between Esther and her sisters, along with photographs of Miriam and Ben.

Esther had started a collection of family photos in her little house, to bring some Cochin into her new life in Israel. There was her wedding photo with Yehuda, flanked by a picture of his parents, and a picture of her parents—taken several years ago on a family excursion—all forming a neat line in the drawing room. Esther often looked at the picture of herself lying on the checked picnic blanket between her parents, laughing at the camera while her mother smiled, a soft drink in her hand, and her father sat in his usual trousers, barefoot, looking slightly odd in his formal attire. Hannah had taken the picture, and Esther had kept her copy of it on her desk in her old bedroom before her marriage, looking at it as she studied. It had given her strength, always making her feel like she had her family, no matter what. She hadn't been able to look at it in the first year of her marriage, but after her sisters re-established contact with her, Esther's memories of her parents weren't quite so painful anymore.

She had had Sarah's engagement photo framed, and even had little Ben's picture proudly displayed with the others. She often pointed it out to Miriam, telling her that the chubby little boy sitting between his parents was her cousin, and that she hoped they would meet and play together sometime. Miriam looked at the pictures with her bright, inquisitive eyes, and Esther wondered how long it took for babies to start recognising people in photographs. The black-and-white faces probably didn't make sense to Miriam yet, but Esther hoped with all her heart that her baby would be able to meet all the people in the photos in real life, too.

***

Dearest Essie, read Sarah's latest letter, *I hope you're doing well.*

Controlling her impulse to read the entire letter at her doorstep, Esther hurried into the house and settled into her favourite armchair with a smile. She looked forward to her sisters' letters—Sarah's especially—they were so vivacious and full of life, and never failed to make her smile. Ever since her sisters had come back into her life, Esther found herself brighter, more energetic, and taking a greater interest in her day-to-day activities. Earlier, she had felt like a machine whenever Yehuda was away on military duty, dragging herself through each day for her daughter's sake, when all she wanted to do was lie in bed, thoroughly exhausted by her loneliness and the weight of her heavy heart. She had lost weight, and had stopped taking pleasure in her appearance like she used to. The only time she would dress up well was when Yehuda was home. However, with at least part of her family restored to her, Esther found her appetite returning to her, and began to style her hair and wear lipstick once more. However, as she read more of her sister's letter, Esther found her excitement ebbing away.

I apologise for the short letter this time, wrote Sarah, *unfortunately, things aren't too good at home. Papa's business isn't doing well, as his partners have decided to emigrate to Israel. Since both of them are shutting shop, Papa is left running the business alone, and well, he isn't exactly young. He's been finding it difficult to manage the whole thing by himself, and has been running into losses.*

We've been trying our best to pull through, budgeting where we can. Mama has dismissed most of the servants—only the maid remains. It's strange to see Mama in the kitchen all day, sweating at the stove instead of meeting her friends like she used to! I've been helping her as much as I can, but as you know, I'm a terrible cook!

We've cut down on the parties, too—we're trying our best to keep the house going, and really don't have the means to throw lavish gatherings and ply the neighbours with food and drink. We are not complaining, but I am worried about Papa. He is under a lot of pressure, and is spending much longer hours at work than he used to, trying to pull things together.

He dismissed most of his staff last week, saying he can no longer afford to pay their salaries. He didn't tell me this himself—I heard him talking to Mama in the kitchen after dinner. It made me realise that I must do more than help Mama at home—I'm thinking of getting a job, so that the entire burden of providing for the family isn't on Papa's shoulders.

I'm going for an interview tomorrow—a school in Ernakulam has put out an advertisement asking for kindergarten teachers. It doesn't require much experience, and I'm hoping I'll get it.

Pray for us, Essie. Pray that we get back on our feet soon.

Love,
Sarah

Despite her newfound vigour, Esther found herself growing restless. Her body was in Israel, but her mind was in Cochin, with her family. It was like an itch she couldn't scratch—like her feet were constantly thrumming, impatient, wanting to go home and do something useful to help her family. Sarah got the teaching job, and for the first time in her life, started to work. If their financial situation weren't so pathetic, it would almost be funny. Sarah had never been the maternal, domestic type, and now she was spending her days teaching toddlers their ABCs and helping her mother with her household chores.

Esther bit her lip, frowning out of her window at the neat, planned landscape of the moshav. Identical houses placed side by side, similar trees sprouting in each backyard, the scorched road turning pale grey, losing its newly tarred sheen under the harsh sun—Israel could not have been more different from Kerala. Yet, when Esther closed her eyes, she saw the lush, wet greenery, the damp roads painted almost black by the rain, the facade of the familiar blue house, its white curtains bright at each window…

She was distracted from her reverie by the familiar ring of the doorbell. Getting up, Esther stretched.

Her slim frame was back to its pre-pregnancy proportions, save for the white slivers that formed a pattern along her belly—the stretch marks that served as a reminder that her body had been home to another human being for nine whole months.

Wondering who was calling on her on a sleepy Saturday afternoon, she opened the door, blinking in the sudden, bright sunlight that poured into her dim living room.

'Mrs Esther Avraham?' asked a young man. Dressed simply in a cotton shirt and brown trousers held up by suspenders, he couldn't have been older than nineteen. Sweat ran down his pale forehead, and he wiped it away with the back of his hand.

'Yes?' asked Esther.

'Telegram,' he said, handing over a small piece of card. Accepting it curiously, Esther asked him to wait while she fetched him a glass of water. The boy gave her a grateful smile, and sat down on her doorstep, looking exhausted.

As she poured him a glass, Esther read the telegram. It was from Sarah. *Papa had a stroke, very ill. Come home.*

***

Four days later, Esther touched down in India, baby Miriam fast asleep on her lap. She had hurried to organise her departure as fast as she could, using almost all her savings from the Cochini food business to buy a ticket to Bombay. She had written to Yehuda, explaining the reason for her sudden visit to India, and had asked him to reply to her home address on Synagogue Lane.

From Bombay, she had a gruelling train journey to Cochin – it was humid, and the torrential rain caused some of the stops on the route to drag out longer than scheduled. Miriam was cranky and fussy—her cheeks turned red and she cried well into the night, not comforted by Esther's rocking and whispers. Fat mosquito bites rose on her little arms and legs, and Esther had to feed her several times to calm her down and get her to sleep. Fortunately, her compartment was full of ladies, none of whom batted an eyelid when she positioned Miriam at her breast, covering herself with a towel.

By the time they reached Cochin, Esther was exhausted. Catching a glimpse of herself in the compartment mirror as she stood up to leave, she saw purple shadows blooming under her eyes. Her curly hair was a mess, and her lipstick was gone. However, she neither had the time nor the inclination to care.

Stepping onto the platform, she hailed a porter, telling him her seat number. As the bow-legged, red-shirted man disappeared into the compartment, she wrapped Miriam's little jacket tighter around her, pulling her cap lower over her ears. The morning air had a nip to it; after the long, strenuous journey, Esther didn't want Miriam coming down with a cold.

Spending the last of her money on a taxi to Synagogue Lane, Esther paid off the porter and leaned back in the seat of the Ambassador, the familiar smell of cheap velvet seat covers and metal door handles filling her nose. As a child, she had always vomited when travelling in an Ambassador car—the smell had never sat well with her.

Taking a sip of water to settle her nausea, she wet her hanky and wiped her sweaty face. Fortunately, Miriam was asleep, undisturbed by the bumping movement of the car.

Since she was going to see her family after more than a year, Esther decided to make herself presentable. Pulling her compact out of her purse, she squinted into the tiny mirror and carefully applied her lipstick, trying not to smudge it when the car jolted over a pothole. Pulling out her pocket comb, she wrestled with her curls, untangling them with her fingers and doing her best to coax them into some semblance of normalcy. She hadn't bathed since the flight, but there was nothing more she could do than dab some perfume at her wrists and neck, and hope it camouflaged the odour of her sweat.

The sun was now a little higher in the sky, and the car turned onto Synagogue Lane just behind Balu, the old fishmonger. Esther couldn't help but smile softly when Balu ignored the honking car magnificently, crying out his plaintive *kooo-ee* that told the surrounding houses that he was near.

As the tall blue house drew closer, Esther's heart began to race. Her eyes were moist, her heart full of the sights and sounds of Cochin. Securing her grasp on Miriam, who was now awake, Esther paid the driver and turned to face the familiar facade of her home.

Home

Esther rang the doorbell, her heart in her throat. She nervously adjusted her position, shifting Miriam to her hip. Miriam was wide awake—thumb in her mouth, big, intelligent eyes taking in the sudden change of atmosphere. Esther bounced her slightly—the movement also helped her work off her own nervous energy.

She rang the bell again, wondering if her family was up yet.

'Coming, coming,' came her mother's scratchy, early-morning voice from the other side. Esther heard the scrape of Miriam's slippers against the floor, and her heart pounded as she heard the old bolt creak free.

The door opened, and mother and daughter stared at each other.

Clad in a white cotton nightie embroidered with tiny blue flowers, Esther's mother had clearly just woken up. Her hair was unruly, and her eyes were still heavy with sleep. Esther could already see the signs of stress that hadn't been there when she had last seen her mother well over a year ago—there were pouchy bags under her mother's tired eyes, her hair was showing a good inch of grey roots, and her mouth sagged at the corners, framed by faint wrinkles.

Mrs Zakiah's eyes widened at the sight of her youngest daughter on her doorstep, immediately losing the last vestiges of sleep. Her gaze slid to the baby in Esther's arms—and little Miriam stared right back at her grandmother, calmly sucking her thumb.

'Sarah told me about Papa's condition,' said Esther, breaking the stunned silence, 'So I came. May I enter?'

Her mother stepped back, giving her room, apparently still too shocked to say a word.

The house was still dark, with only a hint of the early-morning sun filtering through the lace curtains. It looked exactly as Esther had left it over a year ago—the living and dining areas bore no sign of the massive changes that had taken place in the family.

The centre table bore twin photo frames—one bearing a picture of Hannah, Ezra, and Ben, and the other a copy of Sarah's engagement photo—the one she had sent Esther. There was no sign of Esther and Yehuda.

Pursing her lips slightly, Esther decided that the best way to deal with her parents was to be matter-of-fact. Setting Miriam down on the sofa carefully, she went back to the doorstep to collect her two suitcases.

Hauling them in, she asked her mother, 'Is Sarah here?'

The words had barely left her mouth when a familiar pair of legs appeared at the top of the stairs, and Sarah asked, 'What happened, Mama? I heard the doorbell—'

She paused when she saw Esther standing in the living room with a heavy brown suitcase in each hand, and gave a shriek.

Rushing down the stairs, she ran straight into her sister's arms, shouting, 'Essie! I knew you would come!'

Esther dropped her bags and wrapped her arms around her sister's slim frame, hugging her tight. She was laughing, but her eyes were filled with tears. As they dripped onto Sarah's unruly curls, Esther sniffed, and said, 'It's so good to see you, Sarah.'

All the excitement and noise was too much for Miriam, who immediately started bawling from where she was lying on the sofa. Sarah pulled away, turning towards the source of the noise curiously.

But before she could approach Miriam, someone else had reached her.

'Shhh,' whispered Esther's mother, picking up the squalling infant like she was made of glass.

Bouncing the baby gently, she whispered, 'Don't cry, baby, don't cry.'

Gradually, Miriam's tears stopped, and her cheeks faded from an angry red to a light pink. She observed the new person carrying her, clearly unsure about how to feel.

Capitalising on the moment, her grandmother shifted her so that the baby's head rested against her shoulder, and Miriam was cradled close to her body.

'Hush,' she said, rocking Miriam gently, 'That's a good girl.'

Esther and Sarah exchanged glances, their eyes sparkling with tears.

***

Esther let Miriam bond with her namesake as she and Sarah lifted a suitcase each and began lugging them up the stairs.

'It's so good to see you here, Essie,' said Sarah, her eyes bright, 'I didn't expect you to come so quickly!'

Esther flushed, avoiding her sister's beaming face. 'Family is family,' she said simply, as she swung open the door to her old bedroom.

The room was exactly as she had left it in what felt like a previous life—her textbooks stacked neatly on the desk facing the window, her stuffed animals arranged in a row at the head of the bed, and the old cupboard still standing in a corner of the room, the long, discoloured key poking out of the lock.

Dropping her suitcase on her bed, Esther approached her desk, noting that it was covered by a thick film of dust. Reaching between the curtains to open the window, she found the old bolt stiff and rusty between her fingers. It took all her strength to force it down.

'No one's been in here since, you know...' said Sarah timidly.

'I can see that,' replied Esther. Once again, she forced herself to stay calm, and stifled the rising hurt that threatened to spill over. In the year since her marriage, her parents seemed to have done everything they could have to act like their youngest daughter no longer existed.

Turning to her sister, she kept her face smooth and her tone neutral as she said, 'Well, I'd better get dusting.'

***

Exhausted after the long journey and covered with dust after making her room habitable once again, Esther collapsed on the bed. She wanted nothing more than to sleep.

Sarah pulled off the cloth she had wrapped around her own face and put down the cloth duster she had been using to wipe down Esther's desk.

'I suggest you take a bath before you sleep,' she said, 'You've been on the go for more than two days.'

'Yes,' groaned Esther, forcing herself to sit up. Her sore muscles protested their separation from the soft bed, but she ignored them as she got to her feet.

‘Keep an eye on Miriam while I bathe, please,’ she told Sarah as she dug a towel and a change of clothes out of her bag.

‘Which one, your mother or your daughter?’ asked Sarah, her lips twisting into her familiar smirk.

‘Both,’ replied Esther with a chuckle.

***

To say that it was a relief to feel the hot water flowing over her taut, tired body was an understatement. Esther tilted her head back, allowing the water to soak through her curls and run down her back in rivulets, leaving scalding trails as it went.

As she soaped herself, washing off the grime of her long journey, Esther’s thoughts wandered to Yehuda. Coming back to Synagogue Lane had flooded her with memories of him—more specifically, of their courtship. How he used to drive his little moped, parking it at the entrance to Synagogue Lane; how she would sit at her desk every night, pretending to study, but actually waiting impatiently for their daily rendezvous; the sight of him smiling bashfully at her from where he waited across the street, dressed in his neatly pressed shirt and trousers, his hair slick and carefully parted. It never failed to make her smile, the amount of effort he put into his appearance just to talk to her for ten minutes under a dim streetlamp. In those days, he had smelt strongly of Brylcreem and Hamam soap.

Wrapping a thick towel around herself, Esther quickly crossed the corridor and closed her bedroom door, more out of habit than necessity. The top floor of the house had three bedrooms—Hannah's, Sarah's, and Esther's—and a common bathroom for the three of them. As a child, Esther used to rush to her room immediately after bath, for her sisters thought it amusing to lie in wait for her and tease her endlessly, blocking access to her room. In response, Esther had resorted to getting fully dressed before leaving the bathroom, and so her sisters had lost interest in pulling her leg.

Now, of course, only Sarah remained, and she was far too old to ambush her little sister after her bath.

Esther bolted her bedroom door and dressed quickly. Her heart hammered as she combed her damp hair—she couldn't procrastinate any longer.

Smoothing down her simple white dress with her palms, she padded down the stairs. She could hear baby Miriam cooing, and Sarah and her mother talking to her in hushed tones. Smiling to herself, Esther walked past the kitchen, towards the familiar, heavy doors of her parents' bedroom.

The faded doormat that lay at the doorstep was exactly as she remembered it. Pausing, Esther took a deep breath, letting her hand rest on the dull brass door handle. It was time to meet her father.

Papa

Opening the door slowly, Esther cringed at the long-drawn-out creak that filled the quiet hallway. If her father wasn't already awake, the noise would have surely woken him up. On entering the room, the first thing that hit her was the smell. A potent cocktail of medicines arranged neatly on the bedside table was giving off the strong odour that Esther used to call 'hospital smell' as a child. It was indescribable, bringing to mind images of stark, depressing corridors; rows of slouching patients lining the walls; nurses in white clipping about efficiently, their hair scraped back into tight buns, peeling clipboards in their hands.

What a dramatic change, thought Esther, looking around the neatly arranged room. All her life, the room had smelt faintly of her mother's perfume—a floral scented oil, made and bottled in tiny crystal vials by a Muslim family in Fort Cochin who were carrying on the trade of their ancestors.

Esther had been thrilled when her parents had gifted her her own little bottle of perfume when she turned sixteen—she had long coveted the silent, gleaming bottles of attar that lined the shop window like a parade of glamourous Hollywood stars.

Where there had been vases of delicately scented flowers neatly arranged on the bedside table, now stood an army of medicine bottles emitting their choking odour. A wheelchair was parked at the foot of the bed, and right beside the bedside table was a tall rack with an IV drip hooked onto it.

Following the thin, translucent tube of the drip, Esther's eyes settled on her father. Benjamin Zakiah was lying on the left side of the bed, as he had been doing all his married life. His pale skin that had shone pink in better times was now a dull, murky grey. There were heavy pouches of flesh under his bulging eyes, and his face had hollowed, making his long nose all the more prominent. The left side of his mouth was sagging slightly, a line of drool making its way down to his chin. The corner of his left eye as well as his left cheek seemed to be drooping, giving his face a strangely lopsided appearance. His thin arm lay on the white blanket, the IV drip hooked into the protruding green veins that had earlier been barely visible under his fair skin.

'Papa,' whispered Esther, stepping closer to her father. His eyes swivelled to her, and he watched quietly as she approached, pulling a clean white hanky out of the pocket of her dress and wiping the thick line of drool before it dripped onto his nightshirt. He seemed to be studying her, his bloodshot eyes taking in the details of her face, her clothes, with an unreadable detachment.

Esther cleared her throat.

'Sarah told me you suffered a stroke,' she said softly, 'So I came.'

Her father continued to stare, not even blinking. Esther tried again.

'I want to help, Papa, in any way I can. I know things have been tough lately, but with all of us pitching in, we will make things alright. All you need to do is rest, and regain your health.'

There was silence, except for the steady dripping of the IV. Approaching the bed, Esther sat gingerly on the soft covers, taking her father's hand.

'I will be here for as long as it takes for things to get back to normal,' she said firmly, 'And you can't do anything about it. I am going to take care of you, Papa, and the only way to stop me is for you to recover and tell me so yourself.'

Benjamin Zakiah's eyes crinkled at the corners. He seemed to be laughing at his strong-willed youngest daughter.

'Laugh all you want,' said Esther with a small smile, picking up the medication chart her mother had drawn up, detailing which medicine was to be taken at what time, 'You won't get rid of me that easily.'

***

Between themselves, Esther, Sarah, and Miriam Senior worked out a schedule. They divided the household responsibilities and the duties of caring for Mr Zakiah and Miriam Junior, and Esther wondered if, like Sarah, she could get a job, too. Esther and her mother now had something of an undeclared truce between them—while their relationship wasn't back to its pre-Yehuda status, they weren't at war, either. They worked together in silent companionship, talking about practical, day-to-day things when required. Despite the awkward silences that sometimes stretched out between Mrs Zakiah and Esther, the former had no such awkwardness with her granddaughter.

Esther sometimes laughed to herself when she saw her mother playing with Miriam, recalling how she used to worry that her baby would be shunned by her parents. It was quite the opposite—Miriam had her grandmother wrapped around her chubby little finger.

During the day, they took Miriam into her grandfather's room, and it warmed Esther's heart to see his tired eyes light up when he saw the baby. Apart from one incident where Miriam had tried to pull at his IV, she had behaved herself beautifully, and liked to lie beside her grandfather on the bed, sucking her thumb, or trying to fit her toes into her mouth.

Hannah came around almost every day, helping with the household chores and giving their father his medicines. She often brought little Ben with her, who would join baby Miriam on the bed beside their grandfather.

Ben was rather intrigued by his little cousin. Having never seen another baby before, he found her fascinating. They played together almost every day, getting into the occasional fight that would result in both babies dissolving into loud tears, and having to be separated and pacified by their respective mothers. Nevertheless, Esther was pleased—it was almost like Miriam had a sibling, and no matter how busy Esther was during the day, she was never alone.

Hannah's in-laws continued to give Esther the cold shoulder. They dropped in twice a week to visit Mr Zakiah, and Hannah's mother-in-law never failed to look down her nose at Esther or even ignore her altogether, save for some snide comment about how the prodigal daughter had come home for her 'share.' At this point, Hannah would hastily herd her in-laws out the front door, saying they had somewhere else to be, and would visit later. Esther usually ignored the spiteful old woman, gritting her teeth to prevent herself from retorting, but sometimes she found herself dangerously close to snapping.

Yehuda wrote often, and Esther found herself looking forward to reading his letters in the peace of her old bedroom at the end of each tiring day. He was aware of the family's difficult financial situation, and sent part of his salary to them every month without fail. Esther was deeply touched by this gesture and by his kindness towards her family, despite the way they had snubbed him.

The money Yehuda sent, clubbed with Sarah's earnings and further contributions by Hannah and Ezra helped pay for Mr Zakiah's many medical bills and kept the household afloat. Despite frantic budgeting, there was often little to nothing left at the end of the month. Savings and luxurious living had become a thing of the past. Esther found it relatively easy to manage, as she was used to living a more frugal life in Israel, but it was clear that her mother and Sarah were struggling.

Having had plenty of domestic help all her life, Esther's mother developed several aches and pains as a result of all the physical work she was doing. Her petite frame seemed to sag, and her patience ran thin—she snapped at the smallest inconvenience, and often went into a monologue (within earshot of her daughters, of course) about how the lion's share of the work seemed to fall on her shoulders. Sarah had no patience for drama, and sniped at her mother when she went into one of her *moods*, as the girls called them. Often coming home tired from the kindergarten where she taught,

Sarah would groan at the sight of dishes to be washed, or laundry to be done. On such days, she did her work, but not without a thunderous expression that sat rather oddly on her delicate features. Esther privately felt that it was something of a competition between Sarah and her mother as to who could be the biggest martyr. When they argued, they sounded like hissing cats, sparring in sharp whispers so as to not disturb Mr Zakiah.

Esther often felt like snapping at her mother or Hannah's nosy in-laws, but forced herself to keep her mouth shut. In their eyes, she already had a strike against her for marrying a Malabari, and to argue with them on anything would just lead to the melodramatic mothers on either side painting her as a villain, come home to cause more havoc in their lives. On such days, Esther told herself that she would curse to her heart's content in the privacy of her bedroom, but usually had no time to do so, as she fell asleep as soon as her head hit the soft, downy pillow.

***

Over the next month, Esther found her patience with her family wearing thin. While her mother fussed over little Miriam, whom she had taken to calling 'Mimi', she still refused to clear the air with Esther. On a few occasions, when she found her mother in the same room, Esther tried to talk to her and attempt to ease the tension between them, but her mother would immediately hear the fishmonger calling, the telephone ringing, or remember some obscure task she had to do, and rush out of the room, leaving Esther alone with a burning face.

Sarah's own temper was running short as she struggled to balance her work at the school and at home. Not used to dealing with toddlers, she found herself equally charmed by and exasperated with them—more often the latter. As a kindergarten teacher, she considered herself a glorified babysitter, and the school seemed to be increasing her duties since she was one of the few teachers who wasn't married, and was therefore seen as available for longer hours during the day.

By the time she got home in the evening, Sarah would be exhausted, wanting nothing more than dinner, a hot bath, and her bed. However, she rarely had the luxury to relax, and had to throw herself into a series of household tasks.

Sarah and Esther normally got along well, but with tempers fraying all around, they had a couple of blazing rows over things they would have normally laughed at, like tea spilt on the lace tablecloth, or food staying on the stove for too long and burning.

There were times when Esther found her loneliness returning. Despite being in a full, bustling house, her mother was always finding reasons to avoid her, Sarah was either away at school or operating on a short fuse, and Hannah was busy with her own son and in-laws. While Yehuda wrote as often as he could, it was still not the same as having him there with her, in person. Seeing Hannah with her husband and Sarah go out with her fiancé on weekends only made Esther bitter.

Esther felt like she was holding on to the edge of a rock, trying her best not to get washed away with the fierce tide raging around her. Days, weeks—they seemed to pass in a whirlwind, and Esther barely registered significant moments. She was constantly tired—between caring for Miriam and helping around the house, she hardly had any time for herself and wished for one day, just one day, of complete rest.

Sarah's wedding had to be postponed due to their father's ill health, and also (though they didn't like to admit it to her future in-laws) due to the family's pitiable financial condition. There was no way they would be able to throw the grand parties that usually accompanied a Cochini Jewish wedding, and their mother was insistent that Sarah wear a new outfit, not a hand-me-down of hers or Hannah's.

Sarah was quite practical about her wedding having to be postponed, but Esther knew that deep down, her sister felt the pinch. Sarah's fiancé returned to England, where he started working at a law firm, promising to keep in touch and return to Cochin as soon as possible. Some small, petty part of Esther was glad that he had left, since it would mean that Sarah was in the same boat as her. However, guilt followed swiftly—it broke her heart to see Sarah lonely and downcast when she thought no one was looking.

While Sarah's fiancé and his family were well aware of Mr Zakiah's stroke, they had been kept out of the minute details of the family's newly tight financial condition. Mrs Zakiah had too much pride to admit that they weren't living life on the same scale as before, and while it was apparent to their close friends on Synagogue Lane that the family was struggling, they maintained a polite silence, knowing that acknowledging it by offering help would probably lead to awkwardness between the families.

Ezra and Yehuda faithfully sent money every month, and while Mr Zakiah had more or less stabilised, he was still rather weak, and spent most of his time in bed. He had slowly begun to walk, aided by a walking stick in one hand and someone holding the other.

While Esther was pleased to see her father mobile again, his shrunken frame, hollowed cheeks, and the big, veined bags under his eyes made him look like a mere shadow of his former self. He seemed to have aged twenty years in a matter of months, and his thin arms and legs, with wrinkled skin hanging off them, only added to his aged appearance.

Nonetheless, Mr Zakiah's slow recovery gave a great deal of hope to his daughters. Sarah was less snappy when she saw her father sitting in the drawing room when she got home from work, his polished walking stick leaning against his armchair and a plate of cut fruits on his lap. Esther found herself going about her work with renewed energy now that she could see their efforts yielding results. Hannah often came around with little Ben, and the company of his grandchildren seemed to do Mr Zakiah plenty of good. He would sit on the sofa, the babies perched carefully on his lap, Hannah hovering nearby, ready to shift them if they got too heavy for him. However, Mr Zakiah rarely allowed the children to be lifted out of his arms, and would bounce them gently on his lap, his eyes crinkling at their gurgling laughs. When the children got fussy, Grandpa was the one who calmed them, holding them against his thin white shirt and rocking them back and forth.

The family's spirits lifted further when a large package landed up at their doorstep, heavily wrapped, and bearing multiple stamps from England. It was from Sarah's fiancé, Adam Eliyahu. A note had come with it, and Mrs Zakiah handed it to Sarah to read aloud for the family:

My dearest family,

It gives me great happiness to hear that Uncle Zakiah is

doing better. Please accept this small gift from me—I hope it provides you fun and entertainment, and helps Uncle stay in touch with the outside world.

Warmest regards,
Adam Eliyahu

'What is it?' asked Mrs Zakiah curiously as her daughters hauled the package into the house. Once the outer wrapping had been ripped off, Sarah exclaimed in pleasure.

'It's a television set!'

A Television on Synagogue Lane

It didn't take long for the little grey box to become a part of the family. However, Mrs Zakiah was very strict with how often it could be used; she seemed to treat it the same way she jealously guarded her best cutlery, only to be brought out at the appropriate time, otherwise out of bounds—some sort of squat, square deity that sat in a corner of their living room, hidden from view by a delicate lace cover when not in use. Little Ben and Miriam seemed to regard the television with a sort of wariness—given the reverence with which it was treated, they seemed to think it was a live thing, watching them silently from its corner.

The TV was turned on once in the morning, before Sarah left for work, so the family could listen to the news, and then again after dinner, for a spot of relaxation before bed. Mr Zakiah would stump eagerly into the living room, supported by Esther, and position himself right in the middle of the sofa, where he got the best view. His indulgent wife would bring in a plate of cut fruits, and the family would settle down in front of the black and white screen, absorbed in it for the next half hour. The television created quite a bit of interest among the neighbours as well. Every morning, just in time for the news, the toothy smile of the fishmonger would appear at the Zakiahs' living room window. After delivering his catch, he would linger in the doorway till Esther invited him in, and then stand shyly in a corner of the living room, watching the morning news, till Mrs Zakiah began wondering aloud as to when the neighbours would get their fish for the day.

Ever since Mr Zakiah had begun walking, a steady stream of visitors had started pouring into the house. However, ever since word spread that the Zakiahs now owned a television set, the visitors seemed to conclude their conversations with Mr Zakiah rather hastily, following which they would admire the veiled TV set, compliment Sarah on having found such a thoughtful fiancé, and coyly request Mrs Zakiah to show them how it worked.

'It's like we're the circus, and the TV is a performing elephant they're all coming to see!' fumed Mrs Zakiah as she shut the door behind the latest batch of visitors—the curious children of the family next door.

'Maybe we should start selling tickets, or charge an admission fee,' grinned Esther, as she went to switch off the TV.

Her mother half-turned towards her, and Esther saw a

small smile lifting her cheek. That was good. In the months she'd been home, her mother had not exactly been hostile, but had been cool towards her, merely responding with nods and *hmms*. A smile was definitely progress.

The phone rang suddenly, and Esther hurried to answer it.

'Hello?'

'Hello, Essie, this is Hannah.'

'Hannah! Tell me,' said Esther, cradling the receiver between her ear and her shoulder, and craning her neck to see what her daughter was up to. Miriam Junior had been suspiciously silent for a while, and that made Esther uneasy.

'Um, I have a favour to ask, actually,' said Hannah, her tone apologetic.

'Oh?'

'Yes. You see, Ezra has ordered a TV for us, too, but it hasn't been delivered yet. But there's this really important cricket match this evening—don't ask me the details, I have no idea—and he and Father don't want to miss it. So, we were wondering if…?' Hannah's voice trailed off suggestively. Esther rolled her eyes. She had nothing against Hannah and Ezra, but she found it rather hypocritical that her in-laws criticised their family to high heaven for 'letting' their youngest daughter marry a Malabari, and then shamelessly made use of them to watch TV. Even so, the company would probably do Papa good—he was getting bored of being cooped up at home, but wasn't strong enough to go out just yet. Having visitors would cheer him up.

'Sure, tell them they can come,' said Esther with a resigned sigh.

***

'Miriam?' called Esther, going from room to room in search of her daughter. She knew fully well that Miriam couldn't answer, but she responded to familiar voices with gurgles, and Esther was hoping they would guide her.

Miriam wasn't in the drawing room, nor was she in the kitchen with her grandmother. Esther peeped into her parents' bedroom to see if Miriam was with her grandfather, but the room was empty. That was odd. Where could she have gone? She couldn't crawl up the stairs on her own.

Cold fear gripped her heart. Had Miriam somehow crawled out of the house and onto the road while Esther was on the phone? And where had her father gone?

Rushing out of the front door, Esther's breath caught at the sight before her.

Her father was walking slowly in the small space in front of the house, looking strangely tall in his checked lungi and spotless white shirt. He was carrying Miriam, who appeared to be asleep, her plump cheek against his shoulder. His long, veined hand patted her back gently, and he had a strange look on his face that Esther hadn't seen since her childhood. Contentment.

His walking stick was leaning against the door frame, forgotten.

***

The bell rang on the dot of six that evening, immediately setting Esther's teeth on edge. The vultures had arrived.

Plastering a smile on her face, Esther answered the door. First, she saw Hannah's overbearing mother-in-law—short, plump, and wearing a frock more suitable for a party than a simple evening of watching cricket. The smile she gave Esther lasted barely a few seconds, and didn't reach her eyes. She made a beeline for Mrs Zakiah, her flabby arms outstretched in greeting.

Hannah's father-in-law followed, and he had the grace to give Esther a small, apologetic smile for the inconvenience of their visit. She had always thought him the better of the two, but unfortunately, he often went along with everything his wife said in order to keep the peace. He approached Mr Zakiah, grasped his hands, and then settled beside him on the sofa, a look of anticipation on his face as he turned to face the TV.

Hannah walked in with her husband, little Ben in her arms. Leaning forward to kiss Esther on the cheek, she whispered, 'Thank you so much for doing this.' Esther smiled, hugging her sister, and pulling Ben's cheek gently.

Settling in a chair with Miriam on her lap, Esther tuned in to the conversation in the room. Sarah had just emerged from the kitchen with a tray of orange juice, and politely offered it to the guests first. 'I must say you've chosen well, Sarah,' said Ezra's mother archly as she took her glass, 'How nice of your fiancé to give the family a TV as a gift! But of course, he is one of us.'

Esther's eyes flashed to the older woman's face, but she studiously avoided Esther's gaze. As Sarah bent to give Esther her glass of juice, she murmured, 'Don't react. Don't give her any fuel against you.'

Esther said nothing. Taking a sip from the chilled glass, she hoped she would make it through the evening without snapping.

***

The match seemed to drag on and on, and it wasn't long before the sisters retired to the dining room with little Ben and Miriam, taking the much-awaited opportunity to catch up. They hadn't been able to sit together and have a nice, long chat ever since Hannah got married.

'I'm so sorry about my mother-in-law, Essie,' said Hannah anxiously, 'She's like that with everyone, believe me. She thinks she can say what she wants.'

'How do you live with her, then?' asked Esther disgruntledly, combing Miriam's fine curls with her fingers.

Hannah gave a strained smile.

'I try to stay in her good books,' she said.

'Are you happy living like that, though? She's so domineering,' said Sarah, bouncing Ben on her lap.

'Aren't all mothers-in-law domineering?' asked Hannah mildly.

'Not mine,' said Esther, 'She's quite nice, really. A *paavam*.'

Sarah grinned.

'Tell us more about the Avrahams,' she said, leaning forward.

'Well, they're simple and sweet,' said Esther with a fond smile, 'Bava spends his days running the shop, and Umma looks after the house. Yehuda's sister, Reena, has just finished school. She joined college this year—she is studying at St Teresa's College. That reminds me, I owe them a visit. The last time I went to see them was the day after I landed in Cochin.'

The sun filtered through the leaves of the mango tree that bent protectively over the Avraham house in Ernakulam. The old bougainvillea plant crept over the faded front wall, and a soft, golden light glowed in the living room window. The ancient, light-green moped was parked at the gate, as if Yehuda had just come home from the shop. Esther's heart ached—she missed him more than she had thought possible. She hadn't seen him for months, and somehow, letters could never substitute for being able to meet him in the flesh, feel him, look into his eyes…It also felt strange to be visiting his house when he was nowhere around.

Paying the auto driver, Esther adjusted the dupatta of her rose-pink salwar kameez and shifted Miriam onto her other hip. She had dressed in a conventionally Indian outfit, as she had taken to doing in the presence of her in-laws. Not that they had ever hinted that they were uncomfortable with her usual knee-length dresses—she had just noticed that they themselves preferred Indian clothes, and felt it was polite to go the extra mile for them, since they had been so supportive of her and Yehuda.

Ringing the doorbell, she hoped they wouldn't be too upset that she hadn't been able to visit them more often. Her mother-in-law opened the door, dressed in her trademark cotton nightie. Her wiry curls were pulled back into a ponytail, and her face seemed a little more lined than Esther remembered it. Feeling a pang of guilt, Esther stepped forward, and gave her a hug.

'Welcome, *mole*,' said Umma, patting her gently on the back, 'I was hoping you'd come see us soon.'

Esther flushed with embarrassment.

'How is your father?' asked Umma, smiling at baby Miriam and holding out her hands. Esther passed the baby to her, and entered the house.

'He is okay, Umma,' she said, 'He is improving slowly. Very slowly.'

'I suppose it's his age that's also slowing things down,' mused Umma, while Esther nodded, 'We pray for his recovery.'

'That—that means a lot to me, Umma,' said Esther softly. Her father had never done anything to be friendly with the Jews from Ernakulam—as was evident from his past behaviour, he was one of the many Paradesi elders who believed that the Paradesis were the 'pure Jews,' and it was only their community that carried the bloodline of the ancient kings.

Umma smiled, her eyes crinkling just like her son's.

'Come, Bava and Reena will be happy to see you.'

***

Two hours later, Esther felt her cheeks ache with laughter. While she was plied with crisp banana chips, fresh jackfruit slices, and tall glasses of *naranga vellam* straight from their kitchen, Reena kept them all in splits with stories of her classmates from college. Esther wiped her tears, her shoulders still shaking with mirth. For those two hours, she felt like she was transported to the fun and mischief of her own college days, and the stress of her father's ill health seemed to melt away—at least for a little while.

Miriam thoroughly enjoyed all the attention that was being lavished on her by her grandparents and aunt, and blessed them with her gummy grin.

'I think it's time to go home,' said Esther finally, checking her watch, 'I'll need to give Papa his medicines soon.'

Umma got to her feet, rubbing her knees as she did.

'Before you go, there's something I need to give you, *mole*. Come to my room.'

***

That night, in the privacy of her bedroom, Esther carefully unwrapped the boxes her mother-in-law had given her.

Miriam slept peacefully in Esther's old cradle, the peeling white paint carefully touched up by Sarah.

Esther glanced at her, hoping she wasn't disturbed by the rustling of paper.

Lifting the lid of the first box, she gasped softly.

Inside was a beautiful, traditional Jewish dress. The

delicately sewn blouse was yellowing slightly with age, but its beauty was undiminished. Lifting it carefully, Esther marvelled at the exquisite lace cuffs that had evidently been sewn on with great care.

Below the blouse lay a traditional wraparound skirt. The fabric was a thick, rust-coloured silk, clearly expensive. Esther held it to her nose, inhaling the scent of camphor and rose.

On opening the second box, Esther felt sudden tears prick her eyelids. Inside was a beautiful set of solid gold—a pair of heavy earrings and an elegantly crafted necklace that must have cost a small fortune. Lifting it to her neck, Esther glanced into the mirror. The band of gold glittered at her neck, casting a glow over her pale face.

Under the jewellery set lay a piece of folded paper. It was crisp and white—clearly, it had been inserted recently.

Opening it, Esther began to read.

My dear Esther,

I always felt bad that I was unable to give you a proper gift to welcome you into this family, due to the hurried circumstances under which the wedding took place.

I am not giving you these gifts out of guilt—take them from me as a token of love. They belonged to my mother-in-law and then to me. Now, I pass them on to you.

I have no doubt that you make my son very happy—despite the hardships the two of you have endured, I have seen you stand unflinchingly by his side, never doubting, never wavering.

I have grown to love you like my own daughter, and Miriam is the light of our lives.

My blessings are always with you.

With love,
Umma

A Visit from Dr Kurup

'The doctor is coming today,' Mrs Zakiah informed her daughters, 'For Papa's monthly check-up.'

Hannah looked up from where she sat on the sofa, baby Ben on her lap.

'Hasn't he been doing better of late?' she asked, as Ben played with her gold chain. She let him, which surprised Esther. Hannah had always been very particular about her possessions being kept just so. Two years ago, she would have thrown a fit if anyone tangled her precious chains. But then again, Ben was her son. Esther suspected Hannah wouldn't be quite so benevolent if Esther played with her jewellery.

'Yes, he has been,' replied Sarah, knocking on the wooden arm of the sofa, 'All thanks to Essie and Mama. They've been doing most of the work—ensuring he bathes, takes his medicines on time, making sure he gets his exercise…'

Esther glanced at her mother. Mrs Zakiah avoided her gaze, and simply said, 'That's not true, Sarah, we've all been doing our bit.'

'But it is true, Mama,' said Hannah unexpectedly, 'Sarah's been working to support the house financially, and I've been coming around once a day to help where I can, but the lion's share of the work is done by you and Essie. There's no doubt about it. In fact, if Essie hadn't come back from Israel to stay at home and help, I doubt we'd have seen such good results with Papa's recovery.'

'Agreed,' said Sarah, nodding firmly.

There was a pause, which quickly turned awkward as Mrs Zakiah didn't respond to her daughters' statements. Suddenly, it all seemed like too much.

The tight knot which had formed in Esther's chest the moment her family had disowned her seemed to squeeze around her heart, making it difficult to breathe. The room was suddenly stuffy, airless, and her vision blurred with tears.

She swallowed.

'Excuse me,' she said, keeping her voice as level as she could as she got to her feet and rushed upstairs to her bedroom.

***

Esther sat on the edge of the bed, her fingers curled so tight against the frame that her knuckles turned white.

She gritted her teeth, unable to stop the flow of tears coming down her cheeks, thick and fast. *No matter what I do, it will never be enough for Mama*, she thought bitterly, twisting her simple wedding ring round and round her finger without really noticing. *She would probably love me better if I had married a Paradesi boy. It makes no difference whether I help take care of Papa or not.*

Deep down, Esther had always harboured a kernel of hope that one day, she would reconcile with her parents, that they would accept her and Yehuda with open arms. She had always known it would take time for that to happen, but Mama's unchanging, cold behaviour towards her over the past few months had made her realise that no matter what she did, no matter how hard she tried, her mother would never have a change of heart.

The realisation settled in the pit of Esther's stomach like a stone, drawing her spirits down with it. It felt like she was losing her parents all over again.

There was a soft knock on the door, and Esther quickly wiped her tears with the back of her hand.

'Yes?' she asked, trying her best to keep her voice steady.

Hannah's head appeared around the door.

'Essie?' she asked.

Looking at the concern and anguish on her eldest sister's face, Esther felt like bursting into tears all over again. She quickly turned her back, in case her face betrayed her.

'I'll be right out,' she said, fiddling with a pile of freshly washed clothes on her bed, 'I just need to put these clothes in the cupboard.'

'Don't bullshit us, Essie,' came Sarah's firm voice, 'We know you've been crying.'

There was a sudden movement, and a soft groan from Sarah. Hannah had used an old childhood tactic—she had elbowed Sarah hard in the ribs. Esther couldn't help the small smile that escaped her lips.

'May we come in?' asked Hannah softly.

Wiping her cheeks once again, Esther turned to the door with a sigh.

'Come,' she said.

Her sisters closed the door behind them, and sat themselves down on Esther's bed. Hannah took Esther's hands, and gazed earnestly into her eyes.

'We know how hard you've been working, Essie, and Mama knows it, too,' she said, 'It's just that Mama is still so wrapped up in social conventions—'

'Mama is wrapped up in her own head, and nothing else,' butted in Sarah, 'Any normal human being would have overcome their reservations long ago. Essie came all the way from Israel to take care of Papa, and Yehuda is sending money every month, even though we've been nothing but nasty to him. Isn't it shameless to accept his money, but not him?'

For once, Hannah didn't reproach her sister for speaking so bluntly. The sisters sat in silence for a while.

'Well, at least Mama likes Miriam,' said Esther finally, 'I suppose that's something.' Sarah opened her mouth to respond, but she was cut short by Mrs Zakiah shouting up the stairs.

'The doctor is here, come down quickly!'

***

Dr Kurup was a kindly-looking gentleman, around the same age as Benjamin Zakiah. Always dressed in impeccable suits, the doctor's substantial girth and benevolent smile gave the impression of a man satisfied with his life.

One of the most eminent doctors in Cochin, the balding gentleman had known the Zakiahs for decades. Esther remembered how he would smile at the sisters over the golden rim of his glasses—his slight head tilt reminiscent of an indulgent uncle.

When he saw them come down the stairs, Esther noticed that his smile hadn't changed a bit. After exchanging some basic pleasantries, Mrs Zakiah led the doctor to her husband's room. Esther always felt a slight tightness in her chest when she entered her father's sickroom—the collection of medicine bottles and tablet strips on the bedside table, the wheelchair neatly pushed against the wall, the wooden cane within easy reach of the bed, and the overwhelming 'hospital smell' served as constant reminders of how much life had changed. Nevertheless, things were looking up. The wheelchair hadn't been used in several weeks, and the army of bottles on the bedside table had significantly reduced in size. Instead of lying prone on the bed, Papa was propped up against his pillows, his spectacles on the end of his nose, reading the morning newspaper.

'Ah, Kurup!' he greeted the doctor, putting down his paper.

'Good morning, Mr Zakiah. Anything interesting in the news?' asked Dr Kurup as he took out his instruments and set about examining his old friend.

The two chatted throughout the examination, and Mrs Zakiah and her daughters politely slipped away to look after their chores. Except for the early days after Papa's stroke, when the situation was dire and she was anxious for immediate updates, Mama didn't like to hover. She said it made it look like they didn't trust the doctor.

When Dr Kurup emerged, medical bag in hand, Mrs Zakiah came out of the kitchen with an expectant smile, wiping her hands on a dishcloth.

'All fine, Doctor?' she asked, the upward lilt to her voice betraying the carefully concealed anxiety that still lay below the surface.

'More than fine, actually,' said Dr Kurup, taking off his glasses to give them a wipe, 'Mr Zakiah has shown great improvements over the past few weeks, and you and your daughters are to be credited for taking such good care of him. He is still a little weak, but he can regain his strength through daily exercise. He mustn't be overambitious, though. One day at a time. Also, I think he's fit to return to work.'

Acceptance

The dusty shutters rolled up, making the familiar clattering sound that Esther hadn't heard in months. She took a small step back, covering her nose with her hanky.

Benjamin Zakiah didn't step back.

His tall frame encased in a blue checked shirt and grey trousers a tad too loose for him, considering the amount of weight he had lost, Mr Zakiah still struck an impressive figure as he stood in front of the building that housed the family business. His daughters and wife stood beside him, there to support him on the day he returned to work.

'Welcome back, Zakiah *saar*,' greeted Mr Babu of the neighbouring shop as he walked past, 'Good to see you back.'

'It's good to be back, Babu,' said Mr Zakiah, his eyes fixed on the faded sign above the shop. *Zakiah & Co.*

***

Since Esther's great-great-grandfather's time, the Zakiahs had been well-known business people in Cochin. Trading in silks, coconut oil, and spices had been their bread and butter for several years. However, it was Benjamin Zakiah who had set up Zakiah & Co.—one of the biggest general stores in Cochin—that stocked everything from clothes and vegetables to toiletries and other home requirements. For decades, his shop had been the go-to place for the residents of Synagogue Lane, giving them a steady stream of customers.

Other shops had popped up over the years, but none of them were as big and well-known as the Zakiah's. It had also become something of a matter of prestige for the people of Synagogue Lane to shop at Zakiah & Co., one of the oldest family businesses in Cochin.

When the old Jewish community at Cranganore had faced a flood in 1341 that devastated their homes and businesses, several families fled to Cochin to start from scratch. Their resilience and resourcefulness had become a trademark of their community. Cochin's location as one of the major ports of South India had played a major role in helping them re-establish trade with foreign countries. While it was highly likely that it was the early Malabari Jews who had experienced this flood, the Paradesi Jews—who first came to Cochin in 1492 after having been expelled from Iberia under the Alhambra Decree—often spoke of the incident, and had arranged for it to be painted onto a wall of the anteroom of their synagogue.

The anteroom paintings were also a point of dispute between the Paradesis and Malabaris, because the Paradesi Jews had, in one of the paintings, depicted the Jewish hero Joseph Rabban as their ancestor, whereas the Malabaris maintained that he belonged to their community.

Nevertheless, both Jewish communities had a history of escaping tragedy and starting afresh, with great success. Esther wondered if her father would be able to bounce back with the same alacrity as his ancestors.

'Esther?'

Esther blinked, shaken out of her reverie. Her eyes adjusted to the dim light and dust motes hanging in the air. The shop hadn't been opened in ages, and the Zakiahs were in the middle of a major spring-cleaning operation.

'Sorry, Papa,' she said, dipping the mop into the bucket and resuming her work. Benjamin Zakiah approached her, a duster in his hand and a smile on his face.

'No, no,' he said, 'I wanted to have a word with you about something else.' Esther put the mop back in the bucket, and straightened up, puzzled.

She followed her father to his office at the back of the shop, shrugging at her sisters' quizzical glances as she passed. Papa led her into the office and shut the door behind them.

Esther looked around the familiar room. It was perfectly square, with a heavy wooden desk right in the middle. The walls were a pleasant cream, and delicate printed curtains selected by her mother hung at the windows.

Behind the desk was a row of photographs featuring the various members of the Zakiah family who had been involved in the business. The newest portrait was of her father, taken before he fell ill. Esther stared up at the picture, noting the stark difference in Papa's appearance after his illness. It wasn't just the weight loss and the sudden ageing. After his long convalescence, Benjamin Zakiah seemed…softer, somehow. His eyes were no longer as sharp and hawklike as they were in the photograph, and the rigid line of his mouth was more relaxed, more inclined to lift up into a smile. The office was dusty after months of disuse, and the otherwise meticulously neat desk was a clutter of books and papers. Automatically, Esther stepped forward and began arranging them in neat piles. Her fingers grazed cool glass, and she lifted a small, framed photo that was almost hidden by the mess on the desk. It was a black-and-white family picture of the Zakiahs, taken some months before Hannah's wedding. Esther's heart twisted as she stared at it. They all looked so happy.

Mr Zakiah cleared his throat, and she turned around. She was surprised by the open, somewhat vulnerable look on her father's face. He had never been one to express his feelings—

apart from disapproval, of course. His next words nearly knocked her over.

'Esther, I owe you an apology,' he said.

Esther stared at him, not sure if she had heard him right.

Mr Zakiah sighed.

'I've had a lot of time to think over these past few months,' he said carefully, 'And I have come to realise how...unfairly your mother and I have treated you.'

Esther exhaled sharply, leaning against the heavy desk for support. *Was this really happening*?

'You have been the most dutiful daughter to us—dropping everything and coming back to Cochin when you heard I was ill, working so hard to help me recover and to keep the household running...and a few days ago, Hannah told me that your husband has been sending us money all this while, for my treatment. Most men in his position would not have done so, after having been treated so badly by their in-laws. They would have said *good riddance*!' Benjamin Zakiah's lips twisted into a smile as he spoke.

'Falling in love is not a crime, and yet, we behaved as though it was, and practically exiled you from our house, our family. You had every right to turn your back on us after that and focus on your new life, but you didn't. You came back. You continued to give us nothing but love,' said Benjamin Zakiah, stepping forward to take his youngest daughter's hands in his.

She was shocked to see the tears in her own eyes reflected in his.

'We are so lucky to have you, Essie,' said her father, 'And to have Yehuda, too. You have found a man with a good heart. And we owe you both an apology. Can you find it in your heart to forgive us?'

Esther blinked rapidly, but a stray tear escaped her eyes. She stepped forward, and hugged her father for the first time in years.

'Of course, Papa.'

***

That night, as Esther sat on her bed after a bath, combing through her wet hair, she found herself smiling. The weight she had been carrying around ever since her parents had disowned her seemed to have eased slightly.

Her father had never been one for declarations of love and affection; he had always firmly believed that a man must be detached, practical, clinical. His illness must have changed him a great deal for him to actually seek her out and apologise. Esther had never heard her father apologise for anything before.

Papa is a lot kinder now, she thought, putting away her comb and looking into the mirror. Her pale, oval face stared back—a lot thinner than it had been the last time she had taken a good look at it. *I suppose the strain has got to us all*, she thought with a sigh, *thank God the worst is behind us*. She peeped into Miriam's crib, positioned right beside her bed so she could reach her daughter quickly if she woke up in the middle of the night. Little Mimi had fallen into a routine during their months at Cochin, and had taken to sleeping through most of the night.

Esther rested her arms against the crib, watching her daughter with a smile. Mimi's soft lashes curled against her cheek, and her plump lips were slightly parted. Her tiny hands were curled, as if clutching something in her sleep. It was all Esther could do not to give her sleeping child a kiss right then and there.

She sat on her bed, facing the crib, pulling her legs up to her chin. The nights were always the hardest. Lying in an empty bed, far away from her husband, constantly aware of the fact that he wasn't there to watch their daughter go through so many little milestones every week; Esther found herself in a constant state of yearning, of longing—wanting to be with Yehuda, but not knowing when they could be together again.

It suddenly dawned on her that since her father had been declared fit to work again, she was free of her obligations. The realisation hit her like a truck, and she held on to the edge of her blanket, suddenly feeling adrift, untethered.

I suppose I could go back to Israel, she thought, *and be closer to Yehuda.* Yet somehow, the thought of leaving Cochin rankled. She had settled comfortably into her familiar nook among the coconut trees, warm nights and soft splashing of the Arabian Sea—was she ready to give it all up a second time, and go back to the desert?

There was a soft knock on the door, and Esther was jerked out of her reverie. Twisting around on the bed, she almost fell over in surprise when she saw her mother standing in the doorway, a strangely hesitant look on her face.

'Mama,' said Esther, self-consciously pulling her damp hair over her shoulder. Had her mother come to tell her to leave, now that Papa was better?

Mrs Zakiah closed the door gently behind her, and approached the bed. She paused, glancing around her youngest daughter's room—the room she hadn't set foot in for well over a year.

'Is the baby asleep?' she asked unnecessarily. Mimi was clearly fast asleep in her crib, dead to the world.

'Yes,' said Esther, 'She fell asleep an hour ago.'

There was a moment of tense silence. Esther watched her mother twist her hands, and shift her weight from one foot to the other.

'What is it, Mama?' she asked.

Mrs Zakiah took a deep breath.

'I would like you to know that I am sorry for how I treated you and your husband,' she said mechanically, as if she had rehearsed her speech beforehand, 'He has helped us during this tough time, and is clearly…not bad.'

Esther raised her eyebrows.

'He is welcome to our home anytime,' continued Mrs Zakiah, carrying on with her rehearsed speech, 'As is his family. Papa and I look forward to getting to know them.'

Suddenly, Esther saw her mother clearly. After months and months of heartache, of being unable to understand why her mother saw her marriage as a crime against the Paradesi community, Esther understood. She understood that Miriam Zakiah was a woman who had spent her life in a box, believing exactly what she was told, believing it to the point where she had come to feel protective of her small, square world, and resented anything that threatened its harmony. For she was afraid. She was afraid of what lay beyond her boundaries and her petty prejudices. She didn't know a life outside them, and would be utterly lost if she had to rework her entire worldview. She was comfortable where she was—as a child, she had followed her parents, and as an adult, her husband had taken the lead.

As Esther took in the lines of her mother's pale, pampered face, she suddenly felt sorry for her. Mrs Zakiah had never truly known what it was to be free, and to truly live. She had done more during the months of her husband's illness than she had ever done in her life. And now that her husband was well again, Miriam Zakiah would fall back into her familiar world of the Synagogue, evening parties, and the company of the other middle-aged women of Jew Town.

Her mother was simply a child following instructions issued over fifty years ago. She had never stopped to think, to feel, to explore the world for herself. And she probably never would.

'I forgive you, Mama,' said Esther.

Miriam Zakiah's eyes tightened slightly, as if it wasn't Esther's place to forgive. Still, she gave her daughter a stiff smile, which Esther returned.

It's a start, thought Esther, watching her mother leave the room, her duty to her husband done.

Mending Bridges

Esther whistled as she scrubbed away at the dishes, up to her elbows in soap. The sun shone in through the kitchen window, casting a golden glow on the old tiles.

Mornings were her favourite time of the day. It was when she felt most active, and usually dived headfirst into her chores, finishing them off one by one. By afternoon, she started feeling sluggish, and her eyelids started drooping not long after sundown. Her evening work usually went by in a sleepy blur, following which she would practically fall into bed after Mimi was fed and tucked in.

'Good morning,' said Sarah, walking into the kitchen.

Esther turned and smiled. Her sister was already dressed for school in a neat dress and low heels, her hair pulled back from her face.

'Can I help?' asked Sarah, leaning against the kitchen counter.

'No, I'm almost done,' said Esther, 'This is the last of it.'

'You won't have to do this for much longer, you know,' commented Sarah, reaching over and wiping the dishes with a clean towel, 'Now that Papa's working again, I'm sure Mama will bring back the maid and the cook.'

Esther chuckled.

'That'll be a relief,' she said, 'I'll have more time to focus on Mimi.'

'Will you be staying here, then?' asked Sarah, her eyes bright.

Esther paused, setting down the last dish. Now that her work in Cochin was done, she would have to return to Israel. That was the plan all along.

'No, I'll be going back,' she said quietly, rinsing off the dish and handing it to Sarah to dry.

'Oh,' said Sarah softly, 'I understand… I mean, with Yehuda being there and all. I suppose I just assumed that now that things are alright, you would be staying in Cochin.'

Esther shot her a smile.

'Honestly, I wish I could,' she said, drying her hands, 'I like Cochin far better than Israel. Life here is…less of a struggle, you know?'

'So stay!' urged Sarah, grabbing her by the shoulders, 'Can't you get Yehuda to move back here, too?'

Esther shook her head.

'He's in the military, Sarah,' she said, 'He can't just abandon his tenure and come back to Cochin. And I don't feel good about staying in a different country without a valid reason. As long as he's in Israel, I need to be, too. Otherwise, he'll never get to see Mimi—fleeting visits to India during his leave would be too expensive.'

'Hmm,' mused Sarah, watching Esther with clear, thoughtful eyes, 'Looks like you've given this a lot of thought.'

The corner of Esther's mouth quirked up.

'I have,' she sighed, 'Over the past few months, I've realised just how much I like life in Cochin. Things are established here—there's a way of life that we're used to, and we're not constantly on the lookout for attacks from every corner. It's peaceful here.' There was a long pause, punctuated only by the chirping of a bird that had landed on the window sill, looking for scraps.

'I'll miss you, Essie,' said Sarah softly, as she scattered breadcrumbs on the sill. The sisters stood in silence, watching the bird peck away at its meal.

***

A week later—

'Do you have everything you need?' asked Hannah anxiously, hovering at Esther's elbow. 'Yes, yes, don't worry,' said Esther, pushing down the lid of her suitcase, 'I left some things at the house in Israel, too.'

'Good,' said Hannah, though the creases still hadn't left her pretty forehead, 'Will you and Mimi be alright? On the train to Bombay, and then the flight?'

'We'll be fine,' Esther assured her, 'We've travelled alone before, remember?'

'Still,' pressed Hannah, 'I'm giving you some food for the journey, okay?'

'Okay,' smiled Esther.

There was a soft knock at the door, and the sisters turned to see their parents watching them.

'I haven't come upstairs in months,' said Benjamin Zakiah as he strode in, 'This room hasn't changed at all—except for the crib, of course.'

Esther and Hannah moved away from the bed, giving their parents room to sit. There was an expectant pause, during which Mrs Zakiah stared pointedly at Hannah. Understanding that they wanted to be alone, Hannah scurried out of the room, closing the door softly behind her.

'All ready for the journey?' asked Mrs Zakiah, peering at the two suitcases that held Esther's and Mimi's things.

'Yes, Mama,' said Esther, slightly confused. Had her parents come all the way up to her room just to ask if she was ready?

Mr and Mrs Zakiah exchanged looks, and Mrs Zakiah took a deep breath.

'Won't you consider staying, Essie?' she asked.

Esther was surprised—both by the use of her petname, and the slight wobble in her mother's voice. Unlike her father, her mother's apology had been clinical at best, and Esther didn't think that Miriam Zakiah would ever truly take her back into her heart.

'W-what happened?' was all Esther could say, staring at her mother, who was getting progressively more emotional.

'I'm sorry, Essie, I truly am,' said Mrs Zakiah, her voice cracking as she dabbed at her eyes with a pristine white handkerchief, 'I was angry with you for a long time for marrying outside the community, but as the date of your departure got closer, I began to see just how much both you and your husband have done for us. I wish we could have more time together, *mole*. We will miss you and Mimi terribly if you return to Israel. Can't you stay?'

'Mama,' sighed Esther, sitting on the bed and holding her mother's hands, 'I wish I could. I'll miss you all terribly, too—and so will Mimi. She's become so used to playing with little Ben, and being spoiled silly by her aunts and grandparents.'

Mrs Zakiah gave a watery chuckle and Mr Zakiah put his arm around her.

'But as long as Yehuda is in Israel, I have to be there, too,' said Esther, her heart heavy.

Mrs Zakiah nodded, tears still running down her cheeks.

'Come back as soon as you can, okay?' she said, holding Esther's slender face in her hands.

'I will do my best, Mama,' promised Esther as she hugged her mother fiercely, tears pricking at her eyelids.

Back to Israel

When the plane landed in Israel, Esther wasn't sure she could describe exactly how she felt. On the one hand, she was thrilled to be in the same country as Yehuda once again, to be able to meet him, hold him, and make up for all those months apart when their only form of communication had been letters.

On the other hand, she was strangely nervous—it almost felt like she would be meeting him for the first time. Would there be any changes in him? A small voice inside her scoffed at that thought. In all the letters he had written so diligently over the months, his tone had been the same.

He would always be her beloved Yehuda.

Miriam had grown quite a bit in the few months she had spent in Cochin. It never ceased to amaze Esther how quickly babies could grow, especially in the initial months. Miriam had swiftly progressed from lying on her back to sitting up, and then to crawling. She could even stand, provided someone was supporting her. Every night, Esther's heart felt fit to burst when she lay in bed beside her sleeping baby. She took as many photographs of Miriam as she could with her personal camera, so that Yehuda could see every single stage of his daughter's development. Even so, every time Miriam learnt something new, Esther wished her husband were there to witness it himself, and to marvel over it with her. She couldn't wait for Yehuda to see Miriam again, and to hear what he had to say about how much she'd grown.

While she was excited to be back in Israel, there was also a part of her—if she was being honest, a rather big part of her—that wished she didn't have to leave Cochin. It wasn't just because she had reconciled with her parents. There was just something about Cochin—something that lived in the old coconut trees, the salty air that cooled the streets at night, the silhouettes of the ancient houses of Jew Town, the eyes of the khaki-clad autorickshaw drivers, and in the sharp, early-morning call of the fishmonger—that made Cochin feel like home.

And despite having achieved the goal of returning to the land of her spiritual forefathers, despite being among the first generation of Zionists in the country, Esther did not feel the same way about Israel.

As she made her way through the airport in Israel, Esther pushed her longing for Cochin to the back of her mind.

Miriam had started to stir after a short nap, and was looking rather grumpy. Esther hurried to collect her luggage before Miriam started crying, hoping she could feed her in the taxi. The luggage took an unusually long time to arrive, and Miriam began to get fussy. Her cheeks turned red and she screwed up her eyes, moving restlessly in Esther's arms.

Feeling slightly overwhelmed, Esther was relieved when their bags finally arrived and she could rush out to the taxi stand.

'Don't worry, darling, Mama will feed you soon,' she told Miriam as they neared the exit.

There was a throng of friends, family, and drivers waiting to receive the various passengers coming out of the airport. People of all races and ethnicities crowded together, trying to peer past the doors to see if they could spot their loved ones.

Esther smiled. She had always been touched by the affection people showed at airports. People in India were famously reserved with their affections in public, but airports seemed to be the one place where even Indians let go of their inhibitions and showed their love in its truest form.

She would have walked right past the throng if she hadn't spotted a sign with the words Mrs Esther Avraham printed neatly on it. Her eyes travelled from the sign to the person holding it, and her free hand flew to her mouth. *Yehuda.*

***

'So, did you like my surprise?' asked Yehuda in the taxi, bouncing Miriam on his lap. After Esther had given her a quick feed in the car, she had calmed down. Of course, being with her father had contributed to sweetening her mood considerably. She chuckled as he kissed her cheeks, bouncing her on his knees.

'I loved it,' said Esther, giving him a kiss on the cheek, 'I can't tell you how stunned I was to see you!'

'I managed to get a short leave, and decided that there was nowhere I would rather be than with my girls,' said Yehuda with a shy smile. Esther beamed at him.

As soon as she had laid eyes on her husband, she had rushed towards him, moving as fast as she could with Miriam and the luggage. He had met her halfway, enveloping her in a hug that seemed to go on and on.

Even when she pulled away, Esther's free arm remained wrapped around Yehuda's waist. Her eyes shone as she looked up at Yehuda. Gently taking her face in his hands, he kissed her forehead, and then took Miriam in his arms, the baby giggling when he covered her plump face in kisses. He held her close, like his life depended on it.

Esther closed her eyes as the taxi sailed down the road, smiling at the new memory. She couldn't remember the last time she had been so happy.

'I went to visit Umma and Bava,' said Esther, 'They're fine, and miss you. They've sent a lot of your favourite Kerala snacks for you. Reena has joined college, as you know, and seems to be settling in well. Talking to her took me back to my own college days and all the fun I had with my friends. She sends you her love.'

Yehuda grinned. 'Yes, her letters to me are full of news about her classmates and professors—she seems to be quite popular. For that reason alone, I'm glad she's in an all-girls college!'

'I went to an all-girls college, too,' said Esther mischievously, 'But that didn't stop me from starting a relationship with you!'

'Well, then let's hope Reena finds someone as good as me,' said Yehuda with a cheeky grin, earning a light smack on the arm from his wife.

Their laughter filled the little taxi, and the driver smiled.

***

Over the next few weeks, Esther found her life automatically settling back into its old routine—taking care of her little home, working at the catering service, and looking after Miriam. Her old friends welcomed her back with open arms, and several visited her house, bearing gifts for Miriam and remarking at how much bigger she had grown during her months in Cochin.

Esther was amazed to see how the population seemed to have grown while she was away; it was known that migrants were pouring in for various reasons—some to follow their Zionist dreams, and others to escape persecution. Nevertheless, their moshav suddenly seemed a lot more crowded, with several new neighbours in the simple houses, and even more in the tented transit camps. It became increasingly common to see Jews of various races and nationalities living in the same street, with distinct attires, cuisines and languages. Esther often found herself struck by the sheer diversity of the little country, and was getting to know new people at the synagogue practically every week.

One of the Cochini migrants came up with the idea to build a Cochini synagogue, reminiscent of the old one in Jew Town. Not only would it feel like a piece of home, he said, but it would also provide the Cochini Jews with a sense of community. His suggestion was met with enthusiastic agreement from the other members of the community, and it wasn't long before a petition was put forward to the authorities and permission was granted for the building of the new synagogue. Despite the austerities still being observed in terms of rationing, any expression of Jewish culture—such as speaking in Hebrew, setting up Hebrew schools, studying the Torah, and building synagogues was encouraged

Donations were made by practically every Cochini family, and a few were even made by their relatives in India. Hannah's husband contributed handsomely after Hannah read Esther's letter about the construction of the new synagogue out to him, and he and the others from India who contributed were sent letters of heartfelt thanks from the Cochini community in the Negev, along with an invitation to visit the new synagogue when it was ready.

When she walked home from work, Esther liked to pause and watch the construction. Blue and white tiles had been procured for the floor of the synagogue; while they were nowhere near the ancient, artistic beauty of the tiles in the Paradesi Synagogue in Cochin, they were enough to evoke a sense of nostalgia, to remind people of their old synagogue back home. Delicate lanterns of blown glass in red, green, blue, and yellow had been specially made for the ceiling—another reminder of the synagogue back in Cochin.

Esther felt a little thrill every time she spotted something familiar in the new synagogue—it felt like Cochin was coming to Israel.

Since Yehuda was home on leave, he took care of little Miriam while Esther was at work. Esther had initially been a little worried about this arrangement—her father had always demarcated very clear boundaries when it came to men and women in their house—the women cooked and cared for the children, and the men worked to earn a living. However, Yehuda seemed to have no such rules, and delighted in playing with his daughter. Esther was impressed to see him calmly changing dirty diapers with absolutely no whining or expressions of disgust. He even helped out in the kitchen, and Esther made sure to be very demonstrative in her gratitude. Yehuda's leave seemed like an idyllic time in their little household; her relationship with her parents was restored, and they had started writing to Yehuda as well—it seemed like nothing could go wrong.

Esther lay in bed one morning, her arm curled over Yehuda's chest. The early sun filtered in through the window, creating small pools of gold on their white sheets. The weather was perfect and Miriam was still fast asleep in her crib, which meant that her parents had a little more time alone.

Just as Esther snuggled closer to Yehuda, there was a loud rap on the front door. She tsked in annoyance, wondering who on earth had chosen that very moment to bother them.

Giving her an apologetic look, Yehuda slid out of bed, pulling on his pajama bottoms as he headed to the front door. Esther pulled the blanket a little higher over herself and crossed her arms, waiting impatiently for him to return so they could continue what she had in mind.

When five minutes had passed and he still hadn't come back to bed, Esther carefully wrapped the white sheet around herself, and ventured into the living room. The front door was closed, but Yehuda still stood there with his head bent, the lines of his slim, brown back etched clearly in the first rays of the sun.

'What is it?' asked Esther, worried by his posture. She approached him, tripping slightly on the hem of her bedsheet.

Yehuda turned to face her, a telegram in his hand. His face suddenly looked drawn, and his eyes seemed to have lost their light when he said, 'We are facing increasing border disputes with the Arabs in Palestine. I have been called back to duty.'

Fedayeen

A few weeks later—

‘I’ll be back soon, Mimi,’ said Esther with a smile, handing her daughter to Mita.

Mita, her neighbour, was one of the many Cochini women in the moshav. She was a Malabari, and while the pair hadn’t known each other in Cochin, they had become fast friends in Israel.

Like Yehuda, Mita’s husband was also away most of the time, and the young woman often volunteered to babysit Miriam to pass the time. The two had grown quite close, and Miriam flashed Esther a gummy smile as Mita took her.

Esther’s smile grew wider, and she kissed Miriam soundly on each cheek.

‘Thank you, Mita,’ she said gratefully, ‘I’ll come back soon.’

‘Take your time,’ said Mita warmly, ‘That way, I get more time with my little niece, don’t I?’

Mimi chuckled, and Esther and Miriam laughed.

Waving goodbye, Esther set off for the market.

***

The Cochini market was still new, still small, but had a wide range of spices, dried food, pickles, and other items native to Kerala.

Breathing in the heady, familiar scent that never failed to take her back to Fort Cochin, Esther marched purposefully down the street till she found the first thing on her shopping list—papadams.

Ever since she was a child, Esther had had a weakness for the thin, crispy discs of heaven fried in oil that her mother would mash into their rice and curry on Sunday afternoons. Her mouth watering already, Esther bought three packets of papadams, already planning her next meal of rice and curry to go with them.

Next, she proceeded to the spices, to pick up some things for the Cochini restaurant where she worked. Their business had improved greatly, since there was a constant influx of migrants from Cochin and Ernakulam, all of whom greatly missed their familiar home food. Each of the ladies took it in turns to purchase the week's ingredients, and that week, it was Esther's turn.

Just as she was paying the merchant—a kindly old man from Ernakulam with weather-wrinkled skin, she heard a bang, followed by screams.

Whipping around, Esther's eyes widened as she saw men, women, and children running helter-skelter, ducking into the nearest shops for cover.

A group of armed men were standing bang in the middle of the road, dressed in long, loose shirts and trousers, their eyes narrowed against the blazing sun.

'*Fedayeen*s,' breathed the elderly shopkeeper.

'What?' asked Esther.

'From Palestine,' explained the shopkeeper in Malayalam, looking anxiously out of the window.

'They are freedom fighters for their nation. They want to reestablish Arab dominance in these areas.'

Esther didn't know what to say. Her heart was stuck in her throat, pounding hard as the chaos unfolded outside. Everything felt surreal.

The next few moments seemed to pass in slow motion.

One of the *fedayeen*s turned to face the spice shop, raising his gun.

'Get down!' shouted the shopkeeper, flinging his thin, veiny hand across the counter to warn Esther.

Her knees working of their own accord, she dropped to the floor painfully, feeling the papadams crack inside the bag under her.

A shower of glass from the shattered shop window fell over their heads.

Turning sideways, she saw the shopkeeper staring at her, eyes wide. He was crouching under his counter, his skinny arms over his head. His mouth was slack with fear, and Esther could see his yellowing teeth.

Crawling on her belly, Esther reached the shop's back door.

'Don't!' shouted the shopkeeper, but she didn't hear him. There was only one thought in her mind—*Miriam*.

She opened the door, and the sunlight hit her. Blinking, she felt like she was moving through water as she turned, her feet moving sluggishly. Her knees wobbled, as if they were made of rubber.

Another gunshot sounded, and once again, Esther's body took control. Throwing herself onto the hot concrete, she covered her head with her hands, feeling the shards of glass still clinging to her curly hair. She distantly felt her knees and elbows burn—she had skinned them against the rough, unforgiving surface.

She lay absolutely still—so still that she didn't even realise she was holding her breath. The world was nothing but screams and disembodied legs rushing past her.

Turning her head sideways, she saw more broken shop windows; more people, colliding with each other in confusion, not sure which way to run. People were abandoning their bicycles and mopeds in the middle of the road, letting them fall to their sides as they rushed into shops for shelter.

Looking back, she saw that the shooter had his back to her side of her road. Stumbling to her feet, she ignored the pain in her knees, and forced herself to run in the direction of her house.

Scattered Pieces

Esther shut the door behind her, bolting it with trembling fingers. Shaking, she slid to the floor. Her legs could no longer support her.

Despite the heat of the day, she felt cold. The fine hairs on her arm stood up, and she noticed goosebumps peppering her pale flesh. Her teeth were chattering. The gunshots and the screams of the confused crowd echoed in her mind.

It took her a few moments to realise that she was clutching the strap of her black handbag so tightly that her nails were biting into her palm. Unwrapping her fingers slowly, she saw the little crescent moons left by her nails on the soft, white flesh of her palm. The bag fell from her hand, and landed on the floor with a thud.

Leaning forward, Esther let out a shaky breath, her heart pounding in her ribcage. She raked her fingers through her curly hair, loosening the pins, dark tendrils escaping from her hairdo and falling around her face. Her chest heaved, and she tried to breathe through her mouth in an effort to calm down.

Miriam.

Esther still didn't trust herself to walk. Crawling across the floor on her hands and knees, she reached the telephone table. Pulling the receiver down with shaking hands, she held it to her ear blankly. She couldn't remember the number she was supposed to dial. Shaking her head to rid her mind of the annoying dial tone, she replaced the receiver in its cradle. She took a deep breath, and tried again.

'Hello?'

'M-Mita, this is Esther,' she realised her voice was shaking.

'Esther! Thank God you called! I just heard about the shooting!' said Mita frantically, 'Are you okay?'

'I'm…I'm fine. I made it home in one piece. What about you? Miriam?' asked Esther, feeling close to tears.

'We are fine. Nothing happened here, by God's grace,' came Mita's voice, sounding slightly metallic over the phone.

Esther exhaled, slumping against the wall.

'Thank-thank God,' she stammered, 'If—if it's not a problem, could you please bring Miriam over? I—I can't—'

'Don't worry, love, I understand,' said Mita warmly, 'Just stay where you are. We'll be over in ten minutes.'

'Th-thank you,' Esther managed to say, before replacing the phone in its cradle with a shaky click.

Holding the edge of the wall, Esther pulled herself up, feeling like a newborn doe on shaky legs.

Leaning on the wall, she made her way slowly to the kitchen, heedless of the white plaster dust rubbing onto her sleeve.

Once she reached the sink, she ran her hands under the tap, watching the mud wash away, revealing shallow cuts from when she had fallen onto the rough concrete. Washing them thoroughly with soap, she splashed water on her face, and redid her hair. These little activities had a grounding effect on her, and seemed to bring her back to her senses.

As she walked into the bedroom, she passed a mirror fixed to the wall, and noticed that her face was still deathly white.

Opening her cupboard, she pulled out a clean dress at random. She needed to pull herself together for Miriam, to give the girl a sense of normalcy. Miriam was astonishingly sensitive for her age; if her mother seemed anxious or on edge, she would start to fuss and fidget.

Pulling her dirty floral dress over her head and kicking off her scuffed shoes, Esther dressed herself, her hands growing steadier as she did the buttons down the front of her fresh dress. That was good.

As if on cue, the doorbell rang shrilly through the house.

Smoothing down her wayward curls, Esther padded to the front door, ready to receive her daughter.

The Aftermath

When Esther swung the door open, Mita stood on the other side, holding Miriam. Mita's forehead was a series of worry lines, and her eyes were wide. She quickly looked Esther up and down, as if scanning her for injuries.

'Oh, thank God,' Mita breathed, entering the house. Esther all but grabbed Miriam, hugging her daughter close to her chest, and inhaling the familiar baby smell of her hair that was always inexplicably comforting. Feeling her heartbeat slow down, Esther kissed the child soundly on the cheeks, convinced that after the day's events, she would never let her daughter out of her sight again. True, Miriam had been safe with Mita, but what if the shooters had decided to attack the residential area? What then?

Esther squeezed her eyes shut, suppressing a shiver at the possibilities. She felt extremely exposed.

All this while, the dispute with the Palestinians had seemed far away—a border issue. Now, it was much more real, practically on their doorstep. Esther remembered the dark, haunted eyes of the shooter, the way he had fired his gun at shop windows, breaking the glass. She remembered the chaos, the screams, and how she had fallen to her knees, arms flung over her head to avoid any bullets. Was this what Yehuda faced on a daily basis? She would need to pray much harder for his safety, she thought, and thank God for sparing her life.

Later, as she reflected on the day from the safety of her bed, she would realise, that in a way, it couldn't be helped. The Arabs had occupied the land for years and years before the state of Israel had been formed—was it fair to shut them out, to create a new country for immigrants? But many Zionist Jews argued that Israel was their *fatherland*, so to speak—the ancestral homeland of all those of the Jewish faith. They had been hunted for centuries, forced to move from place to place. Therefore, it was only fair to them that they had at least one country where they felt safe and were in the majority. It was a never-ending debate, one that spanned several years. Sadly, it cost innocent lives on both sides, and kept the eternal risk of violence alive.

Esther bit her lip. Ever since moving to Israel, they had lived under the constant threat of conflict with Palestine. Living a secure, peaceful life in Cochin, she had never had any reason to feel threatened or under attack. During World War II, several young men from Kerala had joined the British

Indian Army and Navy; however, Esther's family had not been directly affected since they had no sons and Esther and her sisters had been in school at the time. Her father's wealth had given them a more or less normal life despite rationing across the country. Later, during Independence, when several politicians had conducted rallies in Kerala and Nehru had even visited the city, her parents had avoided the crowds that had thronged to see them, preferring the quiet monotony of their lives in Jew Town. The Partition that had rocked most of north and north-west India seemed like a faraway event, something they read about in the newspapers and listened to broadcasts about on the radio, but never had to experience in person.

After his visit to Palestine in the 1930s, Abraham Barak Salem, the brown-skinned Jew who had fought to end segregation in the synagogues, had begun to help Jews migrate to Israel. It was described as the promised land, the place where every Jew was destined to live, and 'Salem Kocha', as he was known affectionately, helped people arrange the necessary papers.

Esther had never really thought about where the Jews would stay once they got to Israel. She had always assumed that there would be some sort of accommodation arranged for them by a smiling, benevolent government, ready to welcome them home. It was only after reaching Israel and listening to the chatter of the older ladies alongside whom she worked, whose husbands had served in the military before hers, did she realise that the British had drawn lines through Palestine to carve out separate states for Jews and Arabs, and that many Arabs had had to give up their homes in the area that was to become Israel and leave overnight. It was similar to the Partition of India and Pakistan that had happened around the same time—once again orchestrated by the British.

Esther recalled the faces of the migrants who had left their homes in Pakistan and thronged to Delhi with only the clothes on their back—many accompanied by small children and elderly parents—all bearing a haunted expression that spoke of having seen violence and death at close quarters. Were those haunted-looking men with guns who had opened fire in the street just looking to return to the place their parents and grandparents had lived? Granted, their methods were very different from Gandhi and Salem's preferred satyagraha, but if they were to succeed, where would the Jews go? Many of the Jews who flocked to Israel had been imprisoned in concentration camps during the Holocaust and had lost family to the cruelty of Nazi Germany. The Jews, a population that had been hunted and expelled from most countries around the world, had demanded a country of their own, where they would be in the majority and would feel safe. They had initially been offered land in the East Africa Protectorate under the Uganda Scheme, but many Jews had disagreed, pushing instead to return to the fatherland of Israel.

'You look so pale,' said Mita, cutting into Esther's quiet contemplation. Her wiry curls—so reminiscent of the Malabari Jews of Ernakulam—framed her dark, concerned eyes. She rolled up the sleeves of her thin lilac shirt and headed into the kitchen.

'What are you doing?' asked Esther, following her with Miriam.

'Making you a cup of tea,' called Mita, 'And then I'm going to sit with you till you feel better.'

Esther smiled, her heart swelling at this gesture of kindness.

'Thank you, Mita,' she said gratefully, 'But don't let me hold you up.'

Mita gave her a wry smile over her shoulder.

'Hold me up from what?' she asked, 'I am all alone at home. My husband is away at the border, just like yours.'

Esther entered the kitchen, and pulled out a tin of biscuits with her free hand. Emptying some of them onto a plate, she sighed.

'True,' she said, wondering how Mita managed all alone, without even a child to keep her busy.

Esther remembered how her early days in Israel had been the loneliest of her life.

'You can come and stay with me whenever you want,' she said, offering Mita a biscuit. Mita took it with a smile, dipping it into her own cup of tea.

'You might get sick of me,' she said, transferring the teacups to a tray, and carrying them into the living room. Esther followed, carrying Miriam and the plate of biscuits. Of course, Miriam wanted a biscuit, too, so Esther broke off a tiny piece and gave it to her. Little Miriam gnawed on it, getting it wet and sticky. Her teeth hadn't fully come in yet, but she liked to gnaw on things with her gums. Esther suspected she was teething, and often gave her a clean handkerchief to chew on when she saw her getting fussy.

'I won't get sick of you, Mita,' smiled Esther, sitting down on a chair with Miriam on her lap, 'We can keep each other company. You can come to the restaurant, too, and see if you'd be interested in working there. It's quite a nice place, with lots of Cochini ladies. You might already know many of them.'

'Do you think the restaurant will stay open, given today's shooting?' asked Mita, looking worried.

Esther's brow furrowed.

'I don't know,' she admitted, 'I'll have to call the ladies and ask. But I understand where you're coming from—it's not likely that people will be back on the streets very soon. They'll want to be careful. So do I.'

Mita nodded, her eyes slipping to baby Miriam, full of concern.

After Mita left, Esther debated whether to inform her family about the shooting or not. She stood at her window, a hand holding the lacy curtain to the side, watching Mita cross the road and reach her doorstep safely. On the one hand, she didn't want her family to worry. Papa had just recovered, and didn't need another stroke. It was crucial to keep things calm and pleasant, so that he could regain his strength.

On the other hand, she knew they would find out anyway. They had many friends from Synagogue Lane who were now settled in Israel, and news of the shooting was likely to spread like wildfire.

Mulling over her options, Esther pulled out her letter pad and pen. She somehow needed to inform her family without worrying her parents. Suddenly, she knew what to do.

Opening the pad to a fresh sheet, she uncapped the pen and began writing.

My dearest Sarah,

Something happened today, but I need you to keep it private…

***

The next day, the telephone rang shrilly in the living room, jolting Esther out of her sleep. Cursing softly, she pulled her watch out from under her pillow. It was four-thirty in the morning. Who could be calling at this time?

Wrapping her old dressing gown around her, Esther walked barefoot to the telephone, hoping to reach it before its shrill ring woke Miriam.

'Hello?'

'Esther? Are you okay?'

'Yehuda!' exclaimed Esther, waking up immediately, 'How—how did you get to call me?'

'We heard there was a shooting in town,' Yehuda said urgently, 'So we were allowed to call our families. What happened, Esther? Are you okay? And Miriam?'

'We're fine, by God's grace,' said Esther, leaning against the wall, 'I had gone to a shop in town, and had asked Mita to watch Miriam till I got back. Miriam was safe, nothing happened in the residential area.'

'You were in town?' asked Yehuda sharply, 'Esther! My God...are you okay?'

Esther bit her lip.

'Yehuda, don't worry,' she said, trying to sound upbeat, 'I dodged—I threw myself to the ground, and kept my head low. Nothing happened to me.'

'You dodged—' Yehuda swore, which was quite unlike him. He was usually very particular about not swearing in the presence of a lady—especially his wife.

'Esther, I—' Yehuda seemed at a loss for words, casting about for the right thing to say. Esther held the phone close to her ear, waiting. She had never heard him so agitated before.

'You could have been hurt. Or worse,' he said, his voice tight, 'And I just can't imagine…oh, God, Essie.'

'Don't worry, Yehuda, nothing happened,' said Esther gently, 'I'm safe, see? And the restaurant will be closed till things are stable again, so I'll be at home. I won't be going out anywhere, and I'll be safe.'

'But what if this happens again?' asked Yehuda, sounding pained, 'What if the shooters come to the residential area?'

Esther didn't know what to say. She wished she could be with him, to reassure him that things would be fine.

'You can't stay indoors forever, either,' said Yehuda, 'Listen—my phone time is almost up. Essie, please listen to me—go back to Cochin. Stay with Umma and Bava, or your family, whoever you want. But take Miriam and go. I don't want either of you to get caught in a shooting ever again, especially when I'm nowhere near. Please listen to me, Esther. I'll write soon. I've got to go now. Bye, I love you.'

The phone clicked, but Esther still held the receiver to her ear, unable to believe what she had just heard.

Shockwaves

ISRAEL RETALIATES!
ISRAELI DEFENCE MOVES AGAINST FEDAYEENS
CROSS-BORDER VIOLENCE ON THE RISE

Esther set the newspaper down on the dining table, massaging her temples. The situation was getting worse by the day.

Fedayeen was a term used largely for Palestinian rebels, or freedom fighters, as the old shopkeeper had explained to her on that fateful day. Tensions between Israel and its neighbours had existed since the state of Israel had come into existence, but there seemed to be a sudden spike in the frequency of the skirmishes.

Israel had also launched attacks on villages across the border, suspecting them of harbouring *fedayeen*s. While there was no way of confirming the exact number, there were definitely casualties on both sides. Tensions ran high in the city—people were on their guard, locking their doors as soon as they entered their homes, always keeping a sharp eye out for signs of an attack. Nobody trusted strangers.

Esther got out of bed every morning with a sense of dread. Even before she brushed her teeth, she would read the newspaper, scanning it for information on what the Israeli Defence Forces were doing. Of course, it didn't give her an exact idea of where Yehuda was, but it helped her feel like she was abreast of the situation. She spent hours beside the silent telephone, orienting all her chores around it. Days passed with no contact from Yehuda, and as she settled into her empty bed every night, Esther convinced herself that no news was good news.

'Don't worry, darling,' she told Miriam, who could now sit upright on her own, 'Daddy will come home soon, and then we will all be together. He is thinking about us every single day.'

Miriam smiled, showing the first traces of milk teeth. Esther blinked back a tear, and jumped when the telephone rang shrilly through the silence of the house.

'I'll be right back, darling,' she told Miriam, dropping a kiss on the girl's head as she rushed to answer the phone. Her heart raced. Could it be Yehuda?

'Hello?'

'Hello, Esther?' came Benjamin Zakiah's deep voice.

'Papa?' asked Esther, astonished.

'Esther, we got your letter this morning,' said her father, sounding worried, 'And we've been hearing about the situation in Israel on the news. You were caught in an attack?!'

Esther cursed under her breath. That Sarah! Her stupid sister had clearly blabbed to their parents about the contents of the letter, which was supposed to be for her eyes only.

'I'm fine, Papa,' said Esther in a high, cheerful voice, 'Nothing happened! We're fine!'

'Esther,' said her father sternly, 'I read the letter. Your sister showed it to us immediately, and I believe she was right in doing so. How could you hide something so important from us?'

Esther sighed. 'I didn't want you and Mama to worry,' she said, 'You have to focus on getting better. And honestly, we're fine. No one was harmed in the attack, Papa.'

'But what if there are more attacks, where you're not as lucky?' asked her father. Esther remained silent.

There was a pause.

'Esther, come home,' said Mr Zakiah. There was something in his voice that Esther hadn't heard before—it sounded almost like a plea.

'I can't, Papa,' she whispered, 'Yehuda is here—he's deployed at the border—and if something...something happens to him, I need to be able to take care of him.'

'My dear girl, I am quite sure your husband would want you home, safe with your family,' said her father shrewdly, a hint of his old sternness creeping into his voice. Esther smiled in spite of herself.

'He did say that, but how can I leave him alone here, for the second time?' asked Esther.

Before her father could respond, she heard a loud, anxious voice in the background. There was a clink of coins, and then her father spoke again.

'Your mother wants to speak to you,' he said, 'We are calling from the new STD/ISD telephone in the post office, and are nearly out of coins. But this isn't the last you've heard from us, young lady.'

Esther smiled weakly at the threat, and listened to her father hand over the receiver to her mother with a resigned air.

'Essie?' said her mother, sounding breathless, 'Oh, my dear child, do you know how much your letter scared all of us?'

'Relax, Mama, Mimi and I are fine,' said Esther, knowing that her mother would overreact anyway. Mrs Zakiah had never been particularly good at keeping calm.

'My daughter got caught in a shooting, and you are asking me to relax?' she screeched.

Esther cringed, holding the receiver a few inches from her ringing ear. Well, when put like that, her mother did have a point.

There was another frantic clinking of coins, and Esther pictured her mother fumbling with her purse, or turning impatiently to her husband for more coins.

'You come home as soon as possible, Essie,' she said, 'We're all so worried about you. You come here, and Mimi can play with Ben every day. Your sisters are here, so you won't lack company. And bring Yehuda, too—I'm sure he can find some work here. I know you wanted to build a life in the land of our forefathers, but it is difficult for a mother to sit back and listen to news of shootings and so much violence in her daughter's city. I want all my children here, with me, so I know they're safe.'

There was a pause as more coins clattered in the background.

'Come back to Cochin, *mole*,' pleaded her mother, 'You can live here comfortably with your husband and child. It is so safe here—no fighting, no border conflicts. People of all religions live together so peacefully. Why would you ever want to give that up?'

Memories

The weak post-shower sun filtered through the leafy branches on Synagogue Lane, glinting on the little puddles lining the road.

A small foot landed in the puddle with a loud splash, and childish laughter rang out. Flecks of mud stained the white lacy socks the girl was wearing, but she didn't seem to care.

'Hannah, come! This is fun!' shrieked Esther. No more than five, the child was dressed in one of the frilly dresses her mother liked so much, her curls wild and the little blue ribbon holding them back almost completely undone.

Standing at the doorway of the blue house, Hannah shook her head.

'I'll get dirty!' she called, smoothing down her pristine frock—their eldest sister had always been elegant and ladylike, even as a child.

'Sarah, come on!' yelled Esther.

Sarah pushed past Hannah, and ran to her little sister. Soon, the pair of them were jumping up and down in the puddles outside their house, streaks of mud lining their chubby legs. Passersby smiled, amused at the antics of the young sisters.

'Come in, Mama will get angry if she sees you getting dirty!' called Hannah, leaning against the door frame. Her sisters ignored her completely, and she rolled her eyes.

'Fine, get into trouble if you want!' she yelled, feeling a little miffed.

A bell tinkled, and the familiar call of the cotton-candy man floated down Synagogue Lane.

Abandoning the puddle, Esther and Sarah followed the sound, running towards the old metal cart pushed by an even older man, his bright eyes crinkled at the corners, toothless grin growing wider as he saw the little girls. Even Hannah couldn't resist the pull of cotton candy, and daintily sidestepped the puddles as she skipped to the cart.

'Hello, ladies! Your usual order?' asked the cotton-candy man, inclining his head at the girls. Thrilled at being treated like grown-ups, they nodded excitedly, watching with big, round eyes as his dark, wrinkled hands set to work. He opened the metal box and dipped a long, thin wooden stick into it, spinning it around and pulling it out with a flourish—a magical cloud of bright pink fluff. Just as he was handing it to Hannah, there came a shout from the blue house.

'Hannah! Sarah! Esther!'

The girls looked at each other, eyes wide.

Hannah pushed the stick of cotton candy into Esther's hands and ran back to the house. Little Esther was rooted to the spot, staring after her sister.

'Girls!' shouted their mother, appearing in the doorway.

Sarah stood protectively beside her sister, holding her hand tightly with sticky fingers.

Mrs Zakiah bustled out of the house, gasping when she saw her two younger daughters.

'Look at the state of you two!' she exclaimed, stepping carefully over the puddles as she made her way to her daughters, 'You've got your new dresses covered with mud! And your socks! I can hardly believe they were white just an hour ago.'

Taking Sarah's arm, Mrs Zakiah clucked at the condition of her daughters' clothes.

'We have to be at the party in half an hour!' she groaned, 'Oh, what will your father say?'

She made to pull her daughters back to the house, but they dug their heels in, tightening their grasp on each other's hands.

'What?' hissed Mrs Zakiah, before her eyes fell on the stick of cotton candy clutched in Esther's chubby hand. The cotton-candy man, who had retreated to a safe distance, looked apprehensive, as if he expected a scolding.

Mrs Zakiah exhaled. Bending down, she looked her daughters in the eye.

'Okay,' she whispered with a small smile, 'But just this once.'

The girls cheered, and the cotton-candy man smiled as Mrs Zakiah walked up to him and dropped a coin into his palm.

***

Twelve-year-old Esther stared at her shoes. She could see her distorted reflection staring back in the polished black leather. Beside her, Sarah sighed.

They had left the synagogue at least half an hour ago, but Mama and Hannah were still in conversation with the other Jewish aunties. Their father stood beside his wife, his slightly vacant smile making it clear that he had mentally checked out of the conversation ages ago. Esther giggled.

'I wish they would hurry up,' muttered Sarah under her breath, 'All this talk of lace and organza and what not…I just want to go home and eat!'

'There's pastel at home,' said Esther, and Sarah let out a moan of longing.

'Hurry up, Mama,' said Esther softly, jiggling her feet from side to side. Mrs Zakiah continued talking about a new dress she was having made, and Hannah smiled sweetly, clearly keen on getting into the good books of the aunties. Esther rolled her eyes. Hannah was taking their mother's advice a little too much to heart.

Mrs Zakiah had recently sat the girls down for a talk on The Importance of Finding Good Husbands.

Key points included ensuring that they were soft-spoken, well-behaved, well-groomed, and highly recommended by the Jewish aunties. Everyone knew that when it came to matchmaking, the aunties had the most clout. If they liked you, they'd bring out the best boys for you to meet when the time came.

Esther caught her father's eye just as he was stifling a yawn. She grinned, and was surprised to see him return her smile. Normally, Papa was quite stern with them, always the picture of propriety and decorum. It appeared that the discussion was boring even him to tears.

Esther patted her tummy, and Mr Zakiah understood. Glancing at Sarah, who nodded vigorously in agreement, he gently placed a hand on his wife's shoulder.

'Sarah and Esther are hungry, shall I take them home and give them something to eat?' he murmured, 'You and Hannah come leisurely, there's no need to rush.'

'Oh,' said Mrs Zakiah, looking surprised. Her husband rarely involved himself in domestic tasks. Looking at Esther's and Sarah's long faces, she said, 'Okay, go ahead. We'll join you soon.'

Exultant, Esther and Sarah waved goodbye to the party of ladies and ran down Synagogue Lane, ahead of their father. They waited impatiently at the door for Papa to catch up, and he laughed as he pulled the house keys out of his pocket.

'I've never seen a hungrier pair,' he said as he let them into the house.

'We also wanted to escape from the aunty crowd,' explained Sarah, going straight to the kitchen,

'They're so boring!'

Benjamin Zakiah's laugh boomed through the house. When he entered the kitchen behind them, Esther couldn't help but giggle. Her father looked so out of place in the neat, organised space that was their mother's domain. Mama's floral apron hung from a hook on the wall—she wondered what Papa would look like in it.

'Er…so, what are we having?' he asked, gingerly lifting the lids of various containers on the counter.

'Pastel,' grinned Esther, as she got three plates out of the kitchen cabinet. Like everything else selected by their mother, the plates, too, had a floral design—a procession of tiny pink roses curved daintily around the edge of each porcelain plate.

While she and Sarah laid the table, their father followed them, container of pastel in hand. He gingerly served them, and then himself.

As the three of them sat down to their meal, Esther experienced an unusual sense of familiarity with her father—almost as if he were their friend. Alone with his two younger daughters, he seemed to have stepped out of the 'strict father' persona they were used to. It was…interesting, but even then, Esther had known that it was only temporary.

'Leave some for your mother and sister, girls!' cautioned Mr. Zakiah as the trio dug in. Esther looked up for a moment and smiled at this new, friendly Papa. He smiled back.

***

'Hurry up, girls, we don't have much time,' said Mrs Zakiah, fussing with her spectacle case. She wore a dainty, gold-framed pair of reading glasses just on the end of her nose, and Esther often marvelled at how it managed to stay in place.

Their father was already strapped into his seat behind the wheel, his face set in lines of disapproval.

He hated it when the family dawdled and kept him waiting.

He leaned on the horn, and there was a flurry of activity as the girls piled into the car. Esther was last—she had paused to lock the front door before smoothing down her skirt and sliding into the backseat with her sisters.

'Essie couldn't find the key,' said Hannah primly, and Sarah gave her a light kick on the ankle.

'Sorry, Mama; sorry, Papa,' said Esther breathlessly, glancing at the back of her parents' heads. Mama was peering at a shopping list she had pulled out of her purse, and Papa revved up the engine.

'Ten minutes late,' he grumbled as they set off, 'Are we doing your sister's wedding shopping or going on a picnic?'

Esther wisely said nothing.

Their first stop was the jeweller's.

'Now, we have my wedding jewellery, and your grandmother's,' said Mrs Zakiah, 'But we need to get a good diamond set that's just Hannah's, and some gold bangles, too.'

Mrs Zakiah and Hannah seated themselves behind the glass counter, and a salesman came rushing over to them. Esther and Sarah hung back. They knew that once their mother got started on clothes and jewellery, she would forget everything else around her—not even an earthquake would distract her.

'Look at Hannah,' whispered Sarah with a grin.

Hannah, as always, was trying to emulate their mother. Leaning over the glass counter, she was peering at a diamond set the salesman was showing them with all the fervour of an art student studying a painting.

'God, I need sunglasses,' chuckled Esther, 'That set will blind her groom. Shall we tell him to bring sunglasses?'

Sarah snorted and their mother turned, giving them a stern look. The girls sobered up immediately, and pretended to examine a pair of earrings in a glass case beside them.

'Ugh, can you imagine how crazy Mama will go when it's our turn?' said Sarah, 'At least Hannah cooperates with her.'

Esther bit her lip, her smile fading slightly. Given whom she hoped to marry, she doubted her mother would cheerfully drag her off to the jewellery store and start talking about blue diamonds and whatnot. She just hoped her parents would accept Yehuda without too much fuss. She would happily marry him in a potato sack if she could.

'Well, there's still time for that,' said Sarah, oblivious to her sister's inner monologue, 'Till then, let's enjoy these last few months before Hannah gets married. Who knows when the three of us will get to spend time together like this again?'

'Yes,' said Esther wistfully, 'Who knows.'

The Right Decision

Esther opened her eyes. She was in bed, lying on her back, her legs tangled up in the blanket. She glanced to the side. Mimi was still asleep, curled up in her crib, thumb in her mouth.

Esther sighed, blinking away the tears that had pooled into her eyes. They kept coming, sliding off her cheeks and into her hair.

She sat up, burying her face in her hands. Her heart ached, and her shoulders shook as she sobbed into her blanket, doing her best not to wake Mimi.

She felt like she was drowning.

The days were easy—she went to work, taking Mimi with her. Mita had joined the small catering service, too, and the day usually passed in a busy blur with plenty of Cochini women to chat with. But once she got home, the loneliness began. She missed her family, missed the bustle of Cochin, missed *Yehuda*… One of his friends from Cochin had recently made *aaliyah* to Israel, but Esther hadn't yet met him as he was staying far away, and would be joining military duty soon.

She felt utterly disconnected from her family. Daily telephone calls to India were expensive, and letters took ages to arrive.

Ever since Yehuda and her parents had urged her to return to India, she hadn't been able to get the thought out of her head. She had refused, initially, but the more she thought about it, the more appealing it sounded. Yehuda's mandatory military tenure was drawing to a close as well—why did they have to stay in Israel when they could return to Cochin? Her parents had accepted her marriage, finally embracing Yehuda as their son-in-law, so there was no reason to stay away.

Esther had been able to go to the Paradesi Synagogue with her family during her stay in Cochin—she had assumed it was because she was alone, without Yehuda present. However, Sarah had told her in a recent letter that things at the synagogue were beginning to change—this time, it was the son of a prominent Paradesi family who had married a Malabari girl, with his grandfather's support.

Apparently, the family knew the girl's father, and to prevent the new couple from entering the synagogue or staging a walkout would result in a feud with the grandfather, the patriarch of the family, and one of the most influential Jews in the area. The other elders had no choice but to stay quiet and accept the fact that the inner space of the Paradesi Synagogue was no longer the exclusive domain of the white Jews. Not all of them were happy, Sarah had written, but they had no choice.

Esther's lips quirked into a sardonic smile. Good for the new couple, she thought. She wondered if something similar would have happened had she had her family's support from the very beginning. If Papa had supported them, would the elders have left them alone, to maintain the delicate balance of social relations on Synagogue Lane? Would she and Yehuda have merely been subjected to the cold shoulder or a few snide remarks, and not an entire walkout?

We would have probably stayed on in Cochin then, she thought, *but things are getting better now. Paradesis and Malabaris in Israel intermarry all the time. They even marry Jews from other countries who have settled down here. I suppose they have come to realise that in a strange country, all that matters is that you are Jewish. And back home, their parents will have to accept that their bloodline will no longer be purely Paradesi.*

Esther bit her lip, deep in thought. The thought of returning to Cochin was getting more appealing by the minute. She liked Israel, no doubt, and the more progressive mindset amongst the Jewish folk there, but to her, it had been more a place of desperate loneliness than of new beginnings. At least in Cochin, she had her sisters, her old friends, her in-laws…

Heart racing, Esther scrambled out of bed. She padded barefoot to her desk and fumbled in the darkness for her writing pad and pen. Before taking a decision, she would like to discuss it with her husband—now that his compulsory military tenure was almost up, surely, he wouldn't insist on them staying back in Israel? She knew for a fact that he thought of Cochin, too, and missed his family deeply. What if she could convince him to return?

Unscrewing the cap of her fountain pen, she switched on the desk lamp, glancing at the crib to ensure the light wasn't disturbing Mimi.

Pulling her writing pad towards her, she opened a fresh page, a small, hopeful smile creeping onto her lips as she started to write: *Dear Yehuda…*

Homecoming

'Who's coming home today, Mimi?' asked Esther, lifting her daughter out of her crib.

'Da-da!' squealed Miriam, chuckling as her mother bounced her on her hip.

'That's right!' said Esther, carrying Mimi over to the mirror so she could get the full effect of their appearance, 'Daddy is coming back today!'

In honour of Yehuda's long-awaited return to Cochin, Esther had organised new outfits for herself and Mimi to wear when they went to meet him at the railway station when his train came in from Bombay.

Since their finances were still not what they used to be, Esther had bought some dress material from Ernakulam and stitched the outfits herself on her mother's trusty sewing machine. It was a soft, sky-blue fabric that fell prettily, and was also breathable in Cochin's humidity. For Mimi, Esther had made a sleeveless frock with matching bloomers and a headband, and for herself, a sleeveless top which she wore with slim trousers. Her mother had raised her eyebrows when Esther went downstairs in trousers, but Esther didn't care. Yehuda had often expressed his fascination with her shapely legs, and she was planning to give him a little treat.

Her bags were packed and ready. Yehuda had sent over some of his savings, and they had managed to rent a small house for themselves in Cochin, near the ferry. It wasn't much, but it was close to Jew Town, and just across the water from Ernakulam. Esther and Yehuda had agreed that they needed privacy, especially after having been separated for so long. Mimi wouldn't be lonely—their new house wasn't very far from Hannah's, and she could play with little Ben any time she liked.

Esther hoped they could eventually save enough to buy a house of their own—a place to call theirs, a place where Mimi and (hopefully) her future siblings could grow up, a place where she and Yehuda could grow old together. Esther smiled wide at the thought. Everything seemed to be coming together—her family had accepted her marriage, and her husband was finally coming home. She was going to pick him up from the railway station with her in-laws, following which they would proceed to their new home. Esther had managed to get it furnished with the basics, and was looking forward to hosting Yehuda's family for lunch as their very first guests. After lunch, she was sure he would need to rest—the flight from Israel to Bombay, followed by the train journey south to Cochin was sure to have tired him out. It was their dinner plans she was nervous about.

Her father had declared that Yehuda would be invited over to their place for dinner, and that he had 'something important' to discuss with him. Esther had exchanged nervous glances with her sisters, and her mother had done her best to wheedle it out of Papa, but to no avail. Benjamin Zakiah had spent the day stocking up on liquor to serve Yehuda, and wandering around with an infuriatingly mysterious look on his face.

Their newly forged bond had resulted in Ben Zakiah referring to Yehuda as 'my son-in-law'. Esther marvelled at how far they had come—from being barely tolerated in her house, Yehuda's kindness and generosity towards her family during her father's illness had elevated him to the position of the favourite son-in-law.

'How the tables have turned, *alle*?' Sarah had commented earlier that day, when they caught sight of their father personally selecting the fish to be cooked for their dinner. The fishmonger looked surprised to see Zakiah *saar* examining his catch himself, and made sure to extoll the virtues of practically every fish in his basket.

'Looking niiice,' commented Reena, looking Esther up and down when they met at the station,

'And so is my little niece! All matching-matching with her Mama!'

Esther smiled, greeting Umma and Bava as Reena took Mimi from her. Mimi was delighted at all the attention she was getting, and looked her most angelic self as Yehuda's parents and sister cooed over her. Chuckling, Esther checked out the train schedule, and received a jolt. Yehuda's train was ten minutes early.

'Quick, we need to go to Platform 2,' said Esther, pointing to the schedule, 'He's early!'

'Oh, God,' said Umma as they hurried along, 'We are seeing him after so long— we shouldn't keep him waiting!'

They reached Platform 2, slightly out of breath, just in time to see the long, dusty train from Bombay pulling into the station. Passengers were already standing at the door, luggage in hand, looking dishevelled from their long journey. Porters were pushing their way through the narrow doorways, eager to grab the wealthiest passengers. The Bombay train was highly sought-after—people usually went to the financial capital of India to make their fortunes, and rarely returned empty-handed.

As they had spent so much time apart since they had moved to Israel, Esther always felt her stomach fill with butterflies when it was time to meet Yehuda again. They were married and even had a child, for God's sake, but there was just something about their reunions that had the ability to turn her back into the girl at the topmost window of the big blue house, waiting with a fluttering heart for her sweetheart to turn up on his moped.

To find something to do with her hands, Esther took Mimi back, and began bouncing her nervously on her hip. Little Mimi placed her hand on Esther's cheek, and Esther felt a tug of calm within her. She straightened her shoulders and kissed her daughter on the cheek, feeling her nervousness melt away.

She spotted him at the same time Reena shouted, 'There he is!'

Stepping out of the bogie, suitcase in hand, was the familiar, slender frame of her beloved husband.

He looked tired, and the new lines on his young face tugged at her heart.

'*Yehuda*!' she called, unable to help herself.

He looked up, and their eyes met. His face broke into a smile, and suddenly, Esther realised that she was the one who was finally home.

***

The alarm rang shrilly in the dark room, and Esther woke with a start.

Groping around on the bedside table, she turned it off before it woke Miriam. A loud cry from the crib pushed against the bed told her it was too late.

'Come on,' she whispered, gently prodding Yehuda awake, 'Papa has invited us over for dinner. We need to start getting ready.'

Yehuda stretched, pulling Esther towards him as he did. She smiled, kissing his brow in the darkness. After lunch with Umma, Bava, and Reena, Esther and Yehuda had spent some much-needed quality time with Mimi, and then dozed off in the late afternoon.

As she got up to get dressed, Esther felt a contentment in her heart that she hadn't known for a long, long time. The fact that Yehuda was back, and that they didn't have to be separated ever again, was still sinking in.

Yehuda switched on the lights as he got up and joined Esther at the cupboard, hunting for fresh clothes.

'I need to start looking for a job,' he said as he pulled out a clean shirt, 'Now that I'm here to stay, I need to find something to do.'

'There's always Bava's shop,' said Esther, buttoning her floral dress.

'True,' said Yehuda, and paused.

'I sense a "but"', said Esther, running a comb through her thick curls. Yehuda chuckled.

'But, after a military tenure, I don't know if I can go back to working in a small shop,' he said frankly,

'I need something more…challenging.'

'Hmm,' said Esther, picking up Mimi and checking her diaper, 'As long as it doesn't separate us again, I'm fine with that.'

***

They puttered down to Synagogue Lane on their moped, and Esther couldn't help but be reminded of old times. Of course, now there was a third precious person on the bike, safely wrapped in her arms, seemingly enjoying the ride.

Esther had always known that she wanted at least two children. She and Yehuda had discussed it, too, during his leave in Israel. Now that they were together again, maybe they could start trying—once Yehuda found a job, of course.

As she climbed carefully off the moped, Esther filed the idea away to discuss once they got back home.

Yehuda parked the moped, and tucked the keys into his pocket. In the dim light of the streetlamp, Esther could see the nervousness on his face.

She took his hand.

'Don't worry,' she said softly, 'It won't be like the last time we came here together. Things have changed.'

Yehuda nodded, his eyes crinkling as he smiled down at her.

'I know,' he said, leaning down to kiss her forehead.

Esther smiled.

'Ready?'

'Ready.'

***

The front door swung open as soon as Esther rang the doorbell. She had to restrain herself from rolling her eyes—she was quite sure her family had been lying in wait, anxious to make amends. Her mother was first in line.

Mrs Zakiah looked up at Yehuda with a smile. Her eyes searched his face, as if really seeing him for the first time. There was a moment's pause, following which she grasped his hands.

Esther looked down at the contrast of Yehuda's dark, slender hands in her mother's milky ones. 'Welcome, *mone*,' she said, drawing him into the living room.

Mr Zakiah was already on his feet, beaming at Yehuda. His welcome was far less formal.

'My son,' he said, stepping forward and enveloping a surprised Yehuda in a hug, 'Welcome home.'

A delighted smile on her face, Esther glanced across the room at her sisters. They smiled and nodded.

Esther found herself blinking rapidly, fussing unnecessarily with Mimi's dress to hide the tears of happiness pooling in her eyes.

***

'The food is lovely, Mrs Zakiah,' said Yehuda politely.

The whole family—plus Ezra and little Ben—were seated at the table, tucking into Mrs Zakiah's famous non-vegetarian fare.

The house was bright and noisy, and Esther realised this was the closest they had come to having a party since her wedding.

'Thank you, dear,' said Mrs Zakiah with a smile, 'And don't be so formal. You can call me *Mama*.'

Esther smiled into her plate.

Over the course of the evening, she had seen her mother's approval of Yehuda growing. His manners, humility, and obvious love for his wife and child were clearly making an impression on his mother-in-law. Esther could practically see the last of the reserve melt out of her mother's eyes to be replaced by warmth whenever she looked at her youngest son-in-law.

Papa was in his element, laughing and joking with Ezra and Yehuda. The old Benjamin Zakiah had been far more reserved—he usually let the younger men approach him and make the effort to start a conversation. He had believed that a man of his stature mustn't seem too eager, and would wrap himself in an aura of mystery. Esther and Sarah had often joked that Papa was a prima donna in the Cochini Jewish circles. You had to *earn* the right to talk to him. Now, however, his reserve had fallen away. He was more open than Esther had ever seen him—starting conversations, smiling more, and even passing dishes to those who needed them. He was softer, kinder, friendlier. It couldn't have been more apparent how much his period of illness had changed him.

Papa caught her staring at him, and cleared his throat.

'That reminds me,' he said, loud enough for her to hear as he leaned towards Yehuda, 'I've been meaning to ask you something.'

'Sir?' asked Yehuda, looking enquiringly towards the Zakiah patriarch.

'I suppose you must be looking for a job, now that you're back in Cochin,' continued Papa.

'Yes, sir, I am.'

'I was wondering if you would like to join me in my business. Now that I'm back to work, I find myself in dire need of a partner. A man of your temperament would do nicely. What do you say?'

Yehuda's eyes flashed to Esther's, reflecting her surprise. She found herself unable to control her smile.

Glancing at Mama, she saw her mother give Yehuda an encouraging nod.

He turned back to Mr Zakiah.

'Thank you, sir. I would be honoured.'

The Beginning

That evening, Benjamin Zakiah's house saw a party after what had felt like a very, very long time.

Music from the radio mingled with polite chatter and the clinking of the gold bangles of elegant Jewish ladies against glasses of wine. The occasional baritone, accompanied by hearty laughter and spiced by the fragrance of Mrs Zakiah's best Cochini fare filled the air, transporting Esther back to the days before her marriage.

Her father held court, just like in the old days, seated comfortably on his favourite armchair, surrounded by a knot of venerable, middle-aged Jewish men. Judging by the intensity on their faces, they were discussing one of two things—business or cricket.

In another corner, little Ben and Miriam were surrounded by their own set of admirers, being cooed over by plump Jewish matrons, with Miriam Zakiah beaming proudly over her grandchildren. Hannah was dressed in a sea-green sari, and was making her way through the crowd with a fresh tray of snacks—the previous one had been emptied in the blink of an eye. Esther saw her shoot a smile at Ezra, who was leaning against the wall with a drink in his hand, watching his beautiful wife play hostess.

Sarah was being petted and fussed over by some elderly aunts, all crowding around to see her engagement ring and eager to instruct her in the housewifely arts. She squirmed, clearly uncomfortable with their attention.

Taking pity on her, Esther stood up to rescue her sister when the door swung open, and the room fell silent.

It was Yehuda, framed by the doorway, dressed in one of his trademark cotton shirts and neatly pressed trousers. Behind him, Esther could see his parents and sister—good, they had accepted her mother's invitation.

Being the only Malabaris in attendance, there was hesitance written clearly on their faces. Esther started walking towards her husband, determined to make him feel at home, but someone beat her to it.

'My boy, I've heard so much about you from Benjamin,' said old Uncle Joseph, Esther's late grandmother's brother, wheeling himself over to Yehuda. Clasping those dark, slender hands between his own pale, wrinkled ones, he continued, 'Your help played a major role in helping our Ben recover.'

Yehuda looked so surprised as the old man started shaking his hand that Esther would have laughed out loud if she hadn't been on the verge of tears.

'A good man, a good soldier—I heard you worked hard in Israel, welcome, my boy, come in,' said Uncle Joseph, wheeling himself back to allow Yehuda's family to enter.

Esther blinked rapidly, her smile widening as several prominent members of the Paradesi community broke away from their little groups and went over to speak to Yehuda, to welcome him into their midst. She saw his parents exchange surprised smiles, and decided to make an introduction which she felt was long overdue.

Walking up to them, she said, 'Umma, Bava, I would like to introduce you to my family.'

***

Esther sipped her drink, leaning against Yehuda's shoulder. The couple sat on the sofa, keeping one eye on baby Miriam and Ben, and another on both sets of parents, who had been getting to know each other for about an hour now.

There was still some formality, some reticence in the air, especially from Yehuda's parents. It was not easy to undo centuries of quiet apartheid in a single evening. It would take time for them, as Malabari Jews, to be fully comfortable with the Paradesi community, and to trust that they would be treated with respect and equality. It would also take time for the Paradesi elders to unlearn centuries of prejudice that had been instilled bone-deep in them, right from the time their ancestors had first come to Kerala.

Esther noticed how even though the elders had accepted Yehuda for his role in helping one of their own, they were still treading on eggshells around his family, exchanging stilted smiles. The awkwardness hung heavily in the air, thick enough to cut with a knife.

However, it didn't take long for Sarah to walk across to Yehuda's sister, take her hand, and pull her to her own group of girlfriends from Synagogue Lane. Reena looked pleasantly surprised, and soon fell into an animated discussion with the young Paradesi girls.

'Our generation has hope,' murmured Yehuda, watching his sister, his eyes crinkled at the corners.

'I hope we break down these stupid divisions over the years, and see more marriages like ours,' replied Esther softly, smiling at her husband, 'As it is, the number of Jews in Cochin is dwindling steadily. Everyone is going to Israel. If we refuse to marry outside our communities, we might see a day when there are only one or two Jews left here—a sad fate indeed, considering Kerala has been our home for centuries.'

'That would be sad,' sighed Yehuda heavily, 'Especially since this is one of the few places where we haven't been persecuted. Remember our friends in Israel—those who survived the Holocaust? And the tensions in Israel itself, between the Israeli Jews and the Palestinians. It was so strange, considering how we live in such harmony with the Muslims, Christians, and Hindus here in Cochin.' Esther nodded, her eyes on her young daughter and nephew. The children played on the carpet, secure in their little bubble, completely oblivious to the sounds and smells of the party. Esther smiled.

'We will make a better life for them,' she said to Yehuda.

He smiled at her. 'And till then?' he asked.

Standing up, she took his hand, leading him to the middle of the floor. Tuning the radio, she found what she was looking for—a station that played film songs. Increasing the volume, she turned to him with a smile.

'Till then, we dance.'

Epilogue

It had just stopped raining. Cochin seemed to have been washed clean, its roads gleaming black, and the leaves of the trees no longer a dusty brown but a dark, rich emerald.

Esther inhaled deeply. The smell of the earth just after the rain never failed to calm her, to fill her with a sense of peace. Monsoon was coming to an end, and Esther was making the most of the crisp, rain-scented air before the weather turned.

Resting her hand on Yehuda's shoulder, she held Miriam tightly between them on the old moped as the trio sped off to the Fort Cochin beach. She saw Yehuda's cheek—partially concealed under his helmet—lift in a smile as he felt her light touch.

The beach was unusually peaceful for a Sunday evening. Lifting a gurgling Miriam onto his shoulder, Yehuda walked slowly through the damp sand onto the pier where he had spent numerous evenings with his friends, sharing a cigarette as they listened to the radio, discussing their love lives, or simply lazing, basking in the sun like contented cats.

'*Noku*, Mimi,' he said softly, speaking to his little girl in Malayalam. Her gaze followed his, to the vast blue Arabian Sea, a pale expanse studded with crests of sparkling diamonds.

Miriam followed his gaze, her little thumb in her mouth. The waves reflected in her light eyes, and Esther found herself once again entranced by her daughter's beauty.

A large wave rose up to the pier, crashing onto the aged wood, sending salty droplets of foam everywhere. Miriam laughed, clapping her plump little hands in delight.

'See how she loves the water?' Yehuda told Esther proudly, 'She's a pucca Cochini, this one.' Miriam giggled as a smaller wave lapped against the pier, and Yehuda knelt down. Holding her carefully, he allowed her to dip a hand into the water.

Amazed at her daughter's fearlessness, Esther knelt down beside them as Miriam laughed, her childish squeals drawing smiles from passers-by. The waves seemed gentle as they lapped against the pier, as if they knew there was a baby in their midst.

'Yes, she is,' said Esther softly watching the salty spray rise and fall with every wave that caressed the edge of the pier. A few droplets wet the front of Miriam's cotton frock, but the girl didn't even seem to notice.

Yehuda caught her, laughing, as she made to crawl closer to the sea.

'Rather adventurous, this one,' he laughed, standing up, 'We will have to keep an eye on you, *alle muthu*?'

Miriam giggled, and not for the first time, Esther felt certain that she could understand what they said.

Taking her daughter's little fist, she gently wiped it with the end of her dupatta.

Catching sight of his wife's downcast eyes, Yehuda's smile faded.

'What's the matter, my love?' he asked quietly.

'Nothing,' said Esther, 'I just wonder sometimes if you regret leaving Israel. You worked so hard for us to make *aaliyah*, did so well in the military, and then…'

Yehuda stared out at the sea, a sad smile playing on his lips.

'I don't think *regret* is the right word,' he said slowly, 'I had hoped that it would be a fresh start for us…I wanted our daughter to grow up there. But ultimately, I think we made the right decision for our family's safety and wellbeing. Besides, you never know—maybe the Israel of the future will be different. Maybe it will be a safer, more peaceful place, and Miriam will be able to do what we couldn't.'

Esther stared at her husband's profile, at the wistful longing in his eyes. He turned to her with a smile and swung Miriam up onto his shoulders so she could get a better view of the ocean.

'Whatever happens,' he continued, 'She will have a safe, secure childhood and good memories of Cochin. When she is older, she can decide for herself.'

'She will be just fine,' Esther said softly, smiling up at their apple-cheeked daughter proudly perched on her father's shoulders.

Glossary

Jewish terms

Aaliyah: 'Ascent'; 'to make aaliyah' refers to a Zionist Jew moving to Israel

Bava: Father

Hashem: God

Kippah: A circular cap worn in the synagogue and on religious occasions

Pastel: Fried savoury pastries filled with meat and vegetables

Siddur: Prayer book

Torah: The holy book of the Jews

Umma: Mother

Malayalam terms

Alle: 'Isn't it so?'

Chenda: A large, cylindrical drum

Mole: Daughter

Muthu: Pearl

Naranga vellam: Lemon juice

Noku: 'Look'

Paavam: 'Poor thing', used to refer to someone who is innocent and naïve.

Acknowledgements

This book has been several years in the making. As a child, I was only aware of the existence of Jew Town in Mattancherry—like many others, I thought the Paradesi or 'white' Jews were the only Jews in Cochin. I could not have been more wrong.

When I read *The Last Jews of Kerala* by Edna Fernandes in 2017, my eyes were opened to the fact that there exists another community of Jews in the same city—a larger, older community with a heritage just as rich—that of the Malabari or 'native' Jews, descended from a tribe that emigrated from the Middle East over 2000 years ago. There is also the Meshuchrarim community, who are considered to be either the descendants of mixed-race African-European manumitted slaves who accompanied the Paradesi Jews to India, or those of local Malayali converts who were enslaved. Due to their dark skin and origin, they were at the bottom of the Jewish pecking order in Cochin, unable to gain complete entry into the Paradesi Synagogue and prohibited from marrying the Paradesi Jews. A prominent member of this community, Mr Abraham Barak 'AB' Salem became the first Cochini Jew to earn a law degree, and fought for the rights of the Malabari and Meshuchrarim communities. His son, Balfour, took it a step further, and married a Paradesi Jewish woman—a daring move in those days.

The discovery of these communities also brought with it the sad knowledge that there has been a fissure between the 'white' and 'coloured' Jews for centuries—a silent apartheid that raged in this quiet harbour town, unbeknownst to the rest of the world. My deep fascination with Cochin's Jewish community and its colourful and complicated history resulted in the birth of this book.

There are a few people I would like to thank.

Firstly, Ms Jehanara Wasi for her immediate enthusiasm on reading the first few chapters and for pointing me in the right direction, publisher-wise. Thank you, Ma'am, for being such a good friend and colleague.

Ms Priyamvada K.E., Ms Trisha De Niyogi, and the entire team at Niyogi Books for their belief in my manuscript.

Mr Elias Josephai (affectionately called 'Babu Sir') and Mr Thapan Dubayehudi of Ernakulam—thank you for providing a total stranger with so much historical insight, knowledge, and research resources on your beautiful community and its customs.

Dr Sridevi Menon of the Department of Ethnic Studies at Bowling Green State University, Ohio, for fact-checking my novel and providing her insight on life in Kerala in the 1950s.

My family, for their love and support, and for telling everyone I'm an author when I only mention my day job. Also, thank you for accompanying me on endless visits to Jew Town and the Kadavumbhagam Synagogue to gather information for my research.

My friends, for their support and enthusiasm for every book I write, and for listening to me drone on endlessly about history.

My readers, for picking up this book and deciding to give it a go. If you are ever in Cochin, I highly recommend you visit Jew Town in Mattancherry and the Kadavumbhagam Synagogue on Broadway and learn about Cochin's Jewish history. The Kadavumbhagam Synagogue is over 800 years old and has been painstakingly restored by Babu Sir—it is definitely worth paying a visit to and seeing nearly a millennium of Jewish history!

Last, but not the least—thank you, God.